I0666383

I Was Tortured By the Pygmy Love Queen

First Edition

Jasper McCutcheon

I Was Tortured By the Pygmy Love Queen

First Edition

Published by The Nazca Plains Corporation
Las Vegas, Nevada
2007

ISBN: 978-1-934625-13-2

Published by

The Nazca Plains Corporation ®
4640 Paradise Rd, Suite 141
Las Vegas NV 89109-8000

PUBLISHER'S NOTE
I Was Tortured By the Pygmy Love Queen is a work of fiction created wholly
by *Jasper McCutcheon's* imagination. All characters are fictional and any
resemblance to any persons living or deceased is purely by accident. No
portion of this book reflects any real person or events.

Cover Photos, Antoine Beyeler and Igor Zhorov
Art Director, Blake Stephens

Dedication

To the men of the USS Indianapolis, who truly did suffer perils at sea.

I Was Tortured By the Pygmy Love Queen

Jasper McCutcheon

Contents

Part One – Ain't that a Bitch?

Part Two – Doing My Duty

PART ONE –
Ain't that a Bitch?
A Bit of Background

"It's no good, Carson. You'll never take them off this island."

"I found them didn't I? What's to stop me? You gambled and you lost. Now, get out of my way, old man. Put on your clothes and crawl away to die somewhere else. Don't make me do what I'd prefer not to do."

He's right, you know. I am an old man. I should go home, back to the United States to die in peace. But I cannot die in peace, not there, for I promised myself that my days would end here with these people – people who've given me every joy a man could ever want, people who saved me from certain death.

For sixty years I've kept their secret. For sixty years I've scanned the trade newspapers looking for word of them. For twenty years I've searched the internet for information about them, for word of the inevitable, for news of greedy men and their plans to exploit this hidden-away tribe and the "them" to which Carson and I referred – a commodity of no interest to my ancient friends, but of great value to the rest of the world. Carson is the first, and if I have my way he'll be the last.

Why should I care? It is true that the pygmies did torture me all those years ago when I, Henry Mitchell, was strong and virile and charged with the energy of youth, but as that guy supposedly said, *they know not what they do.* At that time the pygmies were under a spell – the spell of an evil white witch, a westerner like myself, a manipulator unlike anyone else, a full-grown woman who corrupted the pygmies and used them to her advantage. She is the one who truly tortured me, not they.

And so, I've come back not only for them but for myself. This is for the truth of it. It is time for me to tell my true-life adventure as it really happened, but first I've got to take you to the unknown speck of earth where my end began. Come with me to an unnamed island of the Philippines, somewhere near Luzon.

Me and My Grumman

Some people said I was a hero, but during World War II there were plenty of us and most did a hell of a lot more than I did. I was a Navy pilot and my home was the Grumman F4F Wildcat fighter plane. At the Battle of Midway, my buddies and I came off the deck of the USS Enterprise to take on the Japanese fleet, and while we fighters kept the Zeros busy up above Navy dive bombers managed to sink three aircraft carriers that day and another one the next. The Japanese Imperial Navy never fully recovered from that massacre. I had six kills myself, but that's nothing to brag about. One fellow from the Yorktown had 11 and a whole bunch of us pilots got medals. It was the U.S. Navy's way of saying thank you for conducting the first meaningful payback to the Japanese after their attack on Pearl Harbor.

For me, there would be three more years of aerial dogfights and several close calls until 1945 when I got into a serious situation. We were having a quarrel with four battle-weary Zeros when I found myself separated from my squadron. Instantly isolated, I wondered if I'd taken a bullet in my body and drifted into hallucination. One second I'm twisting, turning, maneuvering my Grumman to take pot shots at the enemy, and the next I'm all alone, unable to see any other aircraft friendly or otherwise. But it was no dream. My vision was clouded – clouded by smoke. My forward engine, the one and only engine powering a Wildcat had taken hits.

I never could figure out why the F4F's were called Wildcats. To me, they were more like bulldogs – stubby and rugged, and although Zeros could outmaneuver our Navy fighters the Grumman's tough construction and thick shell made it a machine far superior in stamina and resistance. For this I will forever be grateful to the engineers who designed her and the men and women who built her, because she kept working for me. The same bullets that strafed her motor also knocked out the gauges and radio, so I truly was alone, losing altitude and not liking the looks of the fast-approaching Philippine Sea.

And so, with no hope of or time to find our fleet of ships, let alone my Enterprise flat top, I turned a bit north and a lot west towards the setting sun to seek what I knew to be nearest landfall – the Philippine Islands. My goal was the recently liberated airfield on Luzon and I did sight an island, but five seconds into my silent celebration flames began to shoot from the engine. This wasn't Luzon, nor any part of the Philippines. Tough cookies. Time was up. Sputtering confirmed it. I had to leave her and take my chances on the unknown and tiny island within my sights, so I popped the canopy and said goodbye to my beloved Wildcat. She got me to a spot of earth. I couldn't ask her for more.

As I drifted down from fading sunlight into darkness, the heart-wrenching sound of silence announced her battle was over. Engine dead, she crashed into the sea beyond and took a part of me with her. That fighter plane was the last connection to my ship, to my Navy companions, to the U.S. Navy, and worst of all, to the United States of America, my home. Swallowed by the ocean, my Grumman was gone. So were the chances that anyone from my side would have a clue as to my whereabouts, as to whether I was dead or alive.

The earth welcomed me with arms that brutalized. Floating into a thick tangle of trees, their unforgiving branches and growths scratching my face and hands, poking my limbs and torso, I came to a sudden stop that nearly separated my joints. The parachute was hung up, leaving me suspended in darkness so black that I had no clue as to my distance from the ground. And so I waited for my eyes to adjust. I listened to squawking birds and screeching whatevers protesting my intrusion, until they realized I was no threat and quieted. This left my rapidly-beating heartbeat and heavy breathing as the lone sounds. Eventually, I also settled a bit, realizing that my arrival to this forest could have been much worse.

First, I did a body check, moved both arms and lifted both legs. Everything seemed to work with no pain, no broken bones, no torn ligaments. My face was scratched, as were my hands, a fact known by feel not sight. Such damage would heal itself, but remaining suspended at an unknown height would not. Whatever was keeping me aloft could not be seen and therefore could not be trusted, so I maneuvered myself onto a sturdy, horizontal branch, straddled it and made myself as comfortable as possible. This was not the most cushioned seat I'd ever felt under my tail bone, but would have to do for the night.

After releasing the parachute harness and removing it from my torso, I felt the zipped-shut, right-breast pocket of my flight suit. The topographical map was there but useless until daylight broke, and besides, I doubted that my landing spot had ever been charted anyway, so in the pocket it stayed. So too did the contents of my left pocket – one cigar and a Zippo lighter with which to light it. For tradition, for good luck, this cigar was to be fired up only after my safe return to the USS Enterprise. That celebration could be a long time in coming.

Rather than speculate on where I might be, or whether the human inhabitants of this island, if there were any humans, were friend, foe, or neither, I tried to focus on the good thoughts. Memories of my ship kept me positive, memories of countless celebrations with fellow pilots, many of whom had saved my ass and quite a few who had me to thank for saving theirs. I thought of my bunk mate, Chuck Gibson, and of how proud he had been that very morning when he received his first batch of pictures taken by his wife of their first child. Images of his baby girl remained clear along with the ugly splotches on her angry face. Newborn humans are cute only in the eyes of their parents, but the joy they bring to the mom and dad make all pictures worth a look for the bystander.

My ploy was working. Reminiscing nearly brought dozing, until a rustling below interrupted the process. Clicking sounds followed, which by my estimation were coming from about 30 feet down and all around me. As the clicks changed to high-pitched squeaks, a pricking sensation stung my neck, and thinking it to be an insect I moved to brush it aside with my hand. No insect, it was a fluffy feather. The opposite end was far from fluffy. It was a dart, and removing it from my skin was to be my final act while sitting in my tree-top sanctuary.

Parading the Prize

It's one hell of a thing to wake up from a peaceful slumber to see a dozen daggers pointed directly at you. I was laying on the ground on my back. My flight suit was gone, as was my shirt, which left me stripped to trousers and boots. My hands were pressed between my back and the ground, wrists tied together with something. As for the daggers, they were made of animal bone and held by what at first appeared to be boys, but I quickly realized they were men – men of stunted height, men of near nakedness, men wearing nothing but animal hide wrappings around their loins, men whose loin cloths were filled with man-sized bulges. Their skin was brown; their hair napped. They stood forming a circle around me, crouched and ready. They ranged in height from three-and-a-half to four feet. Their faces were angry, framed by heads too big for their bodies, and like the animals that protested my arrival to their tree, these little men were not pleased to have me in their jungle.

I tried to sit, but two daggers poked my pectorals to suggest I not. Since they seemed to be not in an attack-mode, but more of a holding position as though waiting for something or someone, I laid quietly and scanned my surroundings.

Faint streaks of sunlight pierced through the thick canopy of a rainforest. It came from an angle indicating early or late day. The air, moist but cool, felt of morning. Directly above me was nothing but dark green of massive tree tops, swooping and connecting with one another 60 feet up and beyond. The ground upon which I laid was mostly dirt patched with islands of green moss and sprouts of shortgrass, for I was in a perimeter

– a forest floor clearing surrounded by huts. These structures were made of wood, limbs from trees of the forest covered with foliage from undergrowth, foliage now dead, dried brown and cemented with dried mud. Tiny eyes peered from the openings of these huts, while menacing eyes glared from the dagger-wielding, male pygmies encircling my prone body.

"Usted habla Español? Or English?"

Not even a man of stunted growth could produce such a voice. It was female, fully-grown, confirmed for me as she moved into my view and stood above. Her skin was white and hair blond. She was outfitted in western attire appropriate for a jungle expedition, balloon pants tucked into calf-length, black leather boots and white blouse tucked into the pants. Sitting atop her head was some sort of crown made of animal bone and adorned with black jewels, their glossy sheen sparkling in the vaulted shards of sunlight filtering through forest canopy.

Strangely, the cruel expression on her face did nothing to suppress my slight pangs of elevated masculinity, the odd allure a man senses when he is shirtless before an unknown female, the burning he feels in his breasts as her eyes inspect him, when her gaze drifts to his chest and lingers there a bit too long. Perhaps my state of helplessness triggered this illogical sensation. Perhaps my being denied the touch of any female for nearly eight months can make it seem logical, but whatever fleeting fire I felt or she felt was quickly doused when she planted her boot to the center of my chest with unfriendly force.

I recalled that she'd asked me a question. My reply was standard, the words I'd been trained to say in such situations.

"Captain Henry Mitchell, United States Navy, number 619…"

"Well, well, a Navy man," she interrupted. "A spy, no doubt. Come to destroy my paradise. Is that it?"

She certainly gave me more information than I gave her, and she offered it in a familiar, but unexpected accent - English - of the United States, unmistakably one of the southern states, and I soon heard more of it when I attempted to parrot my sentence.

"Captain Henry..."

"Don't insult me, Captain Henry Mitchell." More of her weight pressed onto my chest as a way to emphasize her displeasure. "The devil himself has sent you here. And to the devil you shall return."

With the removal of her boot from me, the mysterious woman turned to one of her miniaturized, weapon-wielding assistants. "Boban, this man is evil. He must be tested."

Twelve little gremlins attacked. They stripped away my shoes, socks and trousers while kicking and stomping me, some going so far as to jump barefooted upon my prone body. I now was fully exposed for them, my only remaining garment being white briefs quickly turning dirt brown.

With wrists bound behind my back, I defended myself in the only manner possible by barrel-rolling to distance myself. Separation from at least some of them allowed me space to rise onto my knees. If I could stand, I could kick and run, kick and run. With one foot planted I straightened my leg to near-standing, but a pygmy foot kick to the back of my knee buckled it. To the ground I returned where nothing remained for me to do but violently squirm and kick and hope to make contact with something that got in my way.

And so, this pack of little wolves enjoyed playing their game of torment. They darted in to attack me with stomps and kicks while deftly avoiding my flailing legs and air-kicking feet. They laughed about it, and they waited, knowing full-well that eventually I would exhaust myself. I also knew that I would tire, not that it stopped me from kicking. My resistance. My pleasure. My satisfaction that I'd done everything possible to delay whatever test their female Caucasian leader had in mind for me.

I suspect it was a good fifteen minutes before they celebrated their victory by sitting atop my caked-in-dirt, laying-chest-up and gasping-for-air body. Twelve miniature warriors beamed with pride while awaiting further instructions from the mysterious white woman.

"Go, Boban, show our people," she commanded. They rolled me onto my belly, cut the bindings on my wrists, and then grabbed hold my arms and legs to lift me quartered and stretched. "Show them we have captured the devil's disciple."

Her pygmy servants paraded me about the village as though I was a defeated war prize. At the entryway of each hut they stopped to display me – their quarry, stripped, exhausted, humiliated, and I was presented to their bare-breasted tribal women one hut at a time. The females heaped praise upon their male warriors, emerging from each hut upon my arrival. Female hands lifted skyward in gratitude. Dancing and chanting, the women joyfully thanked their brave men for this triumph, this defeated enemy, and my procession circled until every hut was visited, every female emerged to join the celebration.

With my back arched and chest sagging to within six inches of the ground, my parade was painful. Each step taken by my captors sent shockwaves through my spine, but the processional did allow me to further inspect my place of capture and the society into which I was imprisoned. Like the men, female pygmies were covered with loin wrappings of animal hide, but on these coverings where thighs merged to pelvis, an emblem of white was painted - the cross of the Christian faith. Their height averaged the same as the men. A few of the female breasts were round and plump like freshly packaged sausages, but most sagged like tubes of air-leaking, wrinkled balloons. All were disproportionally large, covering not only the lower chest but extending the length of their bellies nearly to their waists.

Huts were spaced approximately ten feet apart. They were arranged in three staggered lines to form a quasi-triangle and I counted 18 of them. The shape of each was a half-sphere, the foundation diameter about 16 feet, the tops forming a dome climaxing eight feet up and their entryway openings two feet wide by three feet tall. Forest tree limbs were bound with strips of animal hide and vine to shape, while dry foliage exteriors were pasted together with dry mud or some sort of compound containing mud.

Behind one line of huts was a clear-water stream that I could hear better than see, while positioned inside one corner of the triangle of huts was a structure shaped unlike the others. It was of greater size, foundation and walls rectangular, dimensions more suitable for full-sized adults and the roof not a dome but more of a wide-degree arc. Leaving no doubt that this structure held special significance, a cross carved of wood was perched upon the apex of the roof, while a stone slab rested on the ground a few feet in front of the entryway. Perhaps a community table, perhaps an altar, its shape was rectangular, and more than likely had once been a mighty boulder, now carved and sanded smooth to shape. Burning embers of a campfire smouldered on the bare ground a few feet in front of the altar. Most earth inside the triangular perimeter of huts was worn bare of growth from countless steps of tiny feet, and the air inside the triangle was motionless, heavy and wet. With each inching upwards of the morning sun the temperature did rise to intensify this heavy air with a heat to open my pores. A flood of sweat quickly dissolved the brown dirt caked upon my skin, as the processional continued to tote the once-again white man round and round the inside perimeter of huts.

In my investigation of the surroundings, in my toleration of the pain, I failed to notice that the white woman had disappeared. Her re-emergence came with a clapping of her hands. The parade route changed directions and moved towards her, stopping with me suspended, chest sagging and hair of my head within her reach.

She stood between the larger hut and stone altar. She stood in different attire. Gone was her jungle expedition look, replaced by her sanctimonious look – a single-garment, cream-colored robe, a red cross embroidered to its middle. With a collarless neck, its circular opening revealed her clavicle bone before gently flowing the length of her body to the middle of her bare calves. Two delicate curves pressed outward to accommodate her healthy breasts. The solid red cross covered her sternum, its vertical stipes extending the area of separation between those breasts, its horizontal patibulum level and aligned above them. It was designed for church choir or church leader. It was meant to be worn over Sunday's best clothing, but this not-unattractive woman was stark naked underneath that thing.

Damn.

She strolled to me. Her feet planted to the earth beneath my stare revealed delicate and slender toes, their nails handsomely trimmed and smoothed but contrasting with the brown of dirt that had stuck to her toes from barefoot travels. The bare of her lower legs was cleanly shaven, her skin soft-looking and vibrant, but just as before, her cruelty quickly destroyed her allure.

"It is time, Captain Mitchell." She clutched the hair on the top of my head, yanking me upwards as far as my neck would allow and bringing my eyes to the level of her robe-covered belly. "Will you renounce Satan and join us in paradise?"

Such meaningless drivel. How could I answer? Even if I was broken down to the point of answering with logic, of answering with effort to save myself from further punishment, there was no logic to any of this. My reply was the same. "Captain Henry Mitchell, United States..."

"You condemn yourself," she interrupted. "You shall be scourged."

Upon hearing the word, females of the tribe bounded into the surrounding forest, giggling as they broke branches from undergrowth and low hanging tree limbs. Their white leader pointed to the altar in communicating her wishes. Pygmy males carried me there. They laid me belly down onto the stone surface while keeping my arms and legs firmly in their grip, spread to four corners and pressed to the altar, and although I doubt that any of them knew it or planned it, my stretching upon the altar was a relief. My spine, so torturously curved backwards for so many agonizing steps, was straightened, my vertebrae obediently snapping back into alignment. Thank you god or satan or whoever's in charge here.

As that pain subsided, the sting of branches brought new torment. Pygmy females carried out my sentence, fresh green growth thrashing my shoulders, back and legs with their assault coming from both sides of the altar. The sting was that of my grandmother. She was the last familial authority to punish her unruly Hank with the dreaded hickory switch, punishment intended for memory more than pain, and as the pygmies flailed upon my exposed skin I realized that their velocity also was symbolic. They hurt but did not damage me. Nonetheless, I struggled with whatever energy I could summon to escape the grips of their male counterparts, my skin slick with sweat wriggling and jerking to nearly break free – to successfully break free with one limb and another for brief seconds. Numbers worked against me. Each faltering grip was replaced by a newly-secured grip until the white woman ordered the men to flip me. Laying on my back, stretched and quartered, my topside was whipped. Pygmy females struck all exposed skin except for my face and the extremities where male pygmy held me in place.

And all this time, my white antagonist stood to my right between the pygmies and the church hut, her hands clasped together palm to palm as though praying for me while the violence she had ordered played itself out upon me until she was satisfied.

"Enough, my children," came the order, and the pygmy females slowly scattered from the altar. I struggled for air, my chest heaving for rapid intakes of laden-with-moisture oxygen. A glaring sliver of sunshine drew a line directly into my eyes and I raised my head first to relieve the glare, and then to inspect for damage to my chest and belly. None was visible, and stranger still, my skin was numb. I felt nothing – no stings from the whipping, no sticking of fabric underwear to my sweat-drenched hips and crotch, not even the grips of my male captors upon my ankles and wrists.

Paralysis? No. I could breathe. I could struggle against my bondage and did so uselessly, but it seemed as though my nerve endings had lost their function, as though my outer shell did not exist. I could see it, but not feel it, and as the white woman commanded her children to cleanse me, the dumping of water-filled buckets onto my prone body changed nothing. The water could have been ice cold or scalding hot. I would not have known the difference.

All other senses were in perfect working order. The white woman approached me, laid her hands upon my chest, and then spoke to her entourage as though I was not there.

"Little ones," she wailed with vibrato. "The devil has sent his servant to do his bidding. He has come to destroy us, but Jesus will protect us. He is our lord and savior. And because we believe in him, we are strong, and we are unafraid. This man must know the suffering of our savior. Only then can he know the love that we feel for him. Only then can he know the joys of eternal life as we do, through Jesus Christ. Amen."

Like parrots, all pygmies seconded her amen, and then with both of her hands raised skyward, this sadistic woman said something rather un-Christian.

"Crucify him!"

Apparently, my innards were unaffected by whatever their branches had done to numb my skin, because I felt sick to my gut. An unseen hand brought a pricking sensation to my neck, the same as experienced in the tree, and for the first time since my capture I spoke words outside my standardized speech, but I mumbled them to myself.

Jesus fucking Christ.

Bliss

The earth from the air is a glorious site. Perched upon my Uncle John's lap, we buzz the clouds in his World War I vintage Curtiss Jenny biplane. Adeline, Illinois and miles of land around it are below. Rows of corn, tan-shucked, nearly ready for harvest; patches of always green forest; grain elevators beside railroad tracks extending as far as my eyes can see, ready to take me east or west whenever I'm ready to leave; and my home, the barn a shiny grey dot of tin-metal roof, the house a smaller grey dot of worn shingles, all are in my singular view. My first plane ride. Up and away from all my problems – no school worries, no dreading of farm chores, the world can go to hell. And what a humongous world it is, thanks to my Uncle John. I love him so. I love being with him, hearing him talk, listening to him tell me of the world beyond Ogle County, inspiring me to dream, to float the clouds with him in control. I'm thinking big, plotting my escape from podunk, listening to every word he says, thankful for what he knows, thankful for what he sees in me, my ambitions, my willingness to learn of other people and other places, and my desire to rise above the mundane...

Splashes of cold water effectively aroused me from my state of tranquility. Yes, the water was cold. I could feel it.

Two parallel trees stood three feet apart between and just to the back side of two huts, and to their trunks I was bound. Two hand-made wooden ladders were leaning upon each tree, which undoubtedly the pygmies had used in order to lift my limp, unconscious carcass to their desired level of height.

My wrists were wrapped in ropes woven of green vines which circled the trees, one wrist secured to each trunk, while the identical method and material bound my ankles, leaving my feet inches from the ground and my four limbs spread into the letter X. The backs of my hands and heels of my feet were flush with the sides of the tree trunks that faced the village perimeter. My fingers, toes and head were free to move, but little else was. Gravity stretched me length-wise, while the flared angles of my arms and legs stretched me side to side.

Below me the tribe gathered to stand with heads bowed, while towering above them planted in the front center of their cluster was the evil female.

And finally, her face.

I could observe her in a straight, unobstructed, downwardly angled line. She could be 30 or 40 or anything in between; no makeup, no lines; eyes of blue, lashes of black; hair of blonde slightly and naturally streaked with tan, its length perhaps to the shoulder but pulled and bound to a pony tail; her lips luscious and pink, thickness one-eighth of an inch, two curves at the cleft, singular curve at the chin; her nose petite, angled upwards for a glimpse of nostril holes, and I was nearly captivated, mesmerized, until she approached me with the palms of her hands clasped together in prayer.

"You must know the suffering of Jesus Christ. Only then will the devil be cast out."

So much for protocols of war. Being quartered and toted about by little devils at least gave me a chance to partially defend myself, at least left me with a remote chance of escape, and despite the humiliation of what I'd so far been through at least the pain of it was minimal. But now my bondage was very real, my fate completely beyond my control, my pain acute and increasing. The absurdity of her supposed reasoning for my punishment, along with the idea that a fellow countryman was doing this to me caused me to swallow her bait.

"Lady, you seem to be a touch misguided. I already know the story of Jesus Christ and this has got nothing to do with him. Are you insane? Or just a manipulator? Hungry for power, hungry for..."

"That is Satan talking," she cut me off. "Boban, silence him."

Her pygmy lackey climbed one of the ladders with a short length of that vine-woven rope in his hand, but I was determined to have my say before the gag came on.

"You abuse the name of Jesus. I don't know what religion this is supposed to be, but it is not Christianity."

"Don't listen my children," she tried to shout above me. "He is possessed of evil."

I increased volume. "Why do you deceive these innocent people? What's in it for you? You crazy bi..."

Boban prevented me from cursing. He forced the short rope between my vile-spewing lips and tied it securely behind my head, which effectively rendered my words unintelligible. As he climbed down and removed all ladders, I said no more, mainly because trying to form words caused the tight gag to cut the corners of my mouth.

From my right came a procession of females, one of whom carried a wooden cross. They were followed by the white woman, who had taken from the stone altar some sort of wooden goblet. She brought it to her mouth and drank, leaving a stain of dark red upon her lips, and then announced the purpose of this ritualistic charade.

"Now we strengthen ourselves against the demon Satan. Come, little ones, drink the blood of Jesus."

Oh, brother was my silent thought. I was unsure as to which pain was greater - hanging in suspended crucifixion or witnessing the hypocrisy surrounding me. The goblet was passed from one pygmy to the next. I could only hope that if indeed they were drinking blood it was the blood of some slaughtered animal, but considering what I'd seen so far the possibility that they had cut themselves to fill their goblet was not so far-fetched. The other possibility that human sacrifices were part of this woman's routine I refused to consider.

For awhile I listened to her meaningless bullshit, asking Jesus to protect them from Satan and to drive the evil spirit from my soul, thus sparing me condemnation to the fiery pits of hell. It was the same brain-warping malarkey I had been subjected to as a child and I did not care to hear any more of it.

Instead, I closed my eyes and gave thanks to what was real. I was grateful to have been raised on my father's Illinois farm. I was glad to have a well-developed body from the hard labor he forced upon me, even though I privately cursed him for it countless times during my youth. I was thankful to have maintained this fit condition throughout my years of service to the Navy, because I would need every bit of that strength to endure whatever tortures this vile woman had in store for me.

The heat was ungodly, sun now at mid-day height, but this came not from the sun. A thick canopy of towering-tree foliage protected the village from all but a few narrow and beautiful, cathedral-like beams. No, this was a tropical heat that enveloped me, the air heavy with moisture and void of motion. I longed for another drenching of cool water from the stream behind me. I could hear its bubbling current, feel the refreshingly cold air its current generated, but it was a tease, too far away to relieve my misery. Also in need of water was my mouth and belly, and I gladly would have accepted some despite my bladder being pressured to release its held-too-long urine.

I had no clue as to how many hours had passed since they plucked me from my tree-top perch. The angle of the sun said early afternoon, but I could only assume it was the day following my night time landing on this slab of earth. For the moment, both the white woman and her pygmy friends were ignoring me. Her "little ones" were staggering about with their arms stretched to the sky and eyes closed, while moaning and crying as though someone had died.

Death would have perhaps been preferable to suffering through the farce being presented below me. The preacher woman began speaking in tongues, that ridiculously comical but irritating babble used by hucksters to convince the gullible of their spiritual superiority. This is god speaking through them, or so goes the claim, but it's just another trick in the arsenal of those who pretend to posses a direct line to the almighty.

This seemed to be an ideal moment for me to relieve myself. That might shut her up, so I let go a long stream and soiled my already dirt-soiled briefs. Ahhhhh! Yes! What satisfaction it gave me to feel my hot urine stinging my legs and dripping off my toes. My bladder gave thanks. Better yet, my action brought about the desired results.

One of the female pygmies saw what I was doing and shrieked in horror, causing the rest of them to stop posturing and drop their jaws in shock. The female shyster, however, was unfazed. In fact, she turned my little act of defiance to her advantage.

"Praise Jesus, my brothers and sisters. Our faith in his power has driven out the first of his evil spirits. Give thanks to our lord and savior. His work has just begun."

A hushed awe fell over the congregation, as they collapsed to their knees, clasping their hands together in prayer. Their lips moved to obediently display their devotion, their reverence for either the woman or her god. I couldn't say which, but I do know her brainwashing techniques were most impressive.

This silent mouthing of praise allowed me to read lips, as I focused on one of the female pygmies near my feet. "Thank you, Jesus," she mouthed. "Praise be to doctor Wilma."

"Ocka Wilwah?" I laughed in my garbled tongue through painful gag. "You gah be ki'ing me!"

The woman in white robe knew exactly what I had said. She instantly transformed her expression from that of the serene minister of goodness to the enraged purveyor of evil. She seemed a bit concerned that her pygmy faithful had also understood my words, but this vile woman knew precisely what to do in case they had. With a restoration of her calm piety, she quickly solved her problem.

"Go, children. Go to your homes. Now we pray in solitude. Pray for the lost soul of this pitiful man. Pray that he too can know the love of Jesus as we do."

Although it was impossible for me to admire this woman, I had to admit that she was a slick one. Not only had she taught them her language, but she also used that language to effectively transform them into robots, and like zombies did they drift towards and into their huts.

Doctor Wilma waited patiently for the last pygmy to disappear before turning her attentions to me. Casually strolling to the stone altar, she lifted a large wooden bowl and brought it with her to me. Water was in the bowl, and Wilma splashed the cleansing liquid onto my groin, watching it cascade down my shorts, legs and feet to wash away my urine.

"I do declare, Mr. Mitchell. You are a disgusting pig."

The gag made it too hurtful for me to speak, but I had to mock her best I could. I repeated with a pained smile. "Ocka Wilwah," which brought nothing more from her than a malicious grin.

She turned away from me, moving towards the hut with steeple on top. Before entering she spun to face me and shook a long-distance fist, but as she did another human of normal height appeared as a shadow behind her, still inside the hut.

The form blocked her path, and when Wilma quickly turned to pass through the doorway, she collided with whoever was standing there.

"Get back, you fool," she barked, and with a violent thrust she forced the shadowed figure inside and out of her way. But before entering, the good reverend lifted the robe above her head and briefly revealed her backside nakedness to me. It was only a five-second glimpse. It came from a distance of at least twenty feet, but it was an effective tease. A bit of pressure bulged my wet underwear, as doctor Wilma disappeared into her hole.

Sebastionized

"Hank, time to get up. Get ready for church."

Ugh. Can there be any words more repulsive to a child? Especially on a frigid, northern Illinois winter's day? There's no school on Sunday, no major chores to do on the farm. Sunday is the one day of the week when a boy can sleep in late under a pile of warm blankets, but that damned church business denies him this pleasure. Don't these religious people know that the body and brain need rejuvenation every once in a while? Why can't they schedule that silly shit in the afternoon? Why can't I just stay at home and talk to god when I feel like it?

The village was silent and I was abandoned to hang from those tree trunks. Drenched in sweat, hungry, thirsty and exhausted, I drifted in and out of sleep during my solitude. For brief minutes I could dream of the past both good and bad, but always awaken to the reality of pain. My poor wrists were charged with supporting most of my weight. The vines wrapped tightly around them and the trees caused numbness in my hands and fingers, so I pumped my fists to draw blood to my hands. The short rope gagging me sliced into the corners of my mouth like a knife. Only by opening my jaw wide could I relieve the pressure, which of course worsened the parched dryness of my tongue and throat.

Of greatest concern was the fact that my breathing had become labored. My suspended weight compressed my chest and diaphragm, causing each inhale to become more shallow than the previous. For relief, I strained my arms and pushed with my heels to lift myself, and then gasped for three huge gulps of air before allowing gravity to resume its punishment.

Pumping my fists for circulation and raising myself for extra oxygen was a requirement about every ten minutes or so. Despite this and the pain of my crucifixion, as Wilma called it, I still was able to doze in between, and with each dozing came the voice of my mother demanding that I get out of bed.

Errol and Helena Mitchell were well-intentioned parents. They always tried to do their best for me and my sisters. Like most, their methods of raising children were derived from their own upbringing, and this church business was merely part of that tradition. In reality, the event itself wasn't so bad, just the getting out of bed when I preferred to sleep late.

Other than water, sleep is what I desired most at that moment, but all reflective thoughts were interrupted by the voice of Boban.

He shouted in a tongue unknown to me, but his words caused all of the men to emerge from their huts toting long, wooden sticks. These were blow guns, the same used to fire the sleep-inducing dart into me when I was sitting in that tree.

As the males gathered in the central clearing, several women emerged with bowls made of wood and placed them atop the stone slab. Each man lined up, took a feathered dart from one bowl, dipped the pointed tip into another and carefully loaded their guns. Once armed, the line of pygmy males marched silently and single file into the rainforest.

As for the females, they assembled with leaf-woven baskets in hand. After a short conference, they scattered, disappearing into thick foliage beyond the village perimeter and in the direction of their stream. Watching these tiny people go about their daily lives gave me a slight distraction from the pain racking my body, but during all the commotion of pygmy activity, I failed to notice that wily Wilma had emerged from the church hut wearing nothing but the crown upon her head. With the two of us alone, she circled behind me and then positioned herself to my left, standing completely naked with hands on hips.

"The air here is thick, don't you think, Mr. Mitchell?" She asked in a sarcastically sweet tone. Her pronunciation of the word "air" was stretched into two syllables, "aayah," as though she were some sort of charming southern belle. Perhaps at one time she had been just that, but no longer.

I lifted myself, flexed my chest and breathed in deep just to show her I still could, as she placed her left hand onto my stomach and rubbed in small circles. Clasping her right hand to the small of my back, she pulled forward and pressed firmly with her left, deep massaging my middle section from just below the rib cage to the waistband of my briefs.

"You are a strong fellow, Henry Mitchell, you truly are, but you don't fool me."

Her fingers slipped under the elastic and I thought for a moment she might peek inside, but suddenly she removed both hands from my body, took the crown off of her head and held it up for me to see.

"Thought you'd steal my treasure, did you?" She instantly reverted to the tone of cruelty, more consistent with her true self. "Is this what you came for?"

Raising my eyebrows, I slowly shook my head to indicate puzzlement and struggled to verbalize through the gag. "Huh?"

"Black pearls... freshwater... extremely rare. There is a bounty here, but you won't get any. They are mine. Do you hear me?"

It was useless to answer, not to mention painful, so I glared and she continued.

"You will tell me how you learned of my pearls. I want to know who else knows. I want to know if somebody sent you or if you work alone."

After returning the crown to perch upon her head, she stalked to the altar and picked up one of those bone-made daggers, and then returned to prop a ladder against one of my trees. Climbing two steps, she carefully slipped the blade between the strip of rope and that little indentation behind my ear. Tugging the blade towards herself, she severed my gag.

"Now, answer my questions."

First, I worked my jaw back and forth to limber it up, and then I told her the truth.

"I don't know black pearls from black coal and don't really care. I'm a Navy pilot. All I want to do is get off this island and back into the air. There's a war going on. Didn't you know that?"

"Liar!" she shrieked, while slapping my cheek with the back of her hand. "You will talk. I rule these little friends of mine and they will do as I say. To them, you are the devil. To me, you are a threat. Until I know if others are coming for my pearls, the pygmies and I are going to put you through hell. You will regret having tangled with me, Henry Mitchell."

Rather than argue, I searched for answers myself, "Who are you? What island are we on and how did you get here?"

Again I was rewarded with a slap to the face, "My name is Wilma Huckabee. Do you find that amusing? Good, choke on it, because it's all you will ever know. Now, tell me the truth."

"Lady, I've told you the truth. My plane was shot up and I had to bail out. This is where I landed. That's all there is to it."

"All right, Captain Henry Mitchell, big man, we'll just see how strong you are. Run your mouth all you like. My pygmies will never believe a word you say. You can suffer or you can talk. The choice is yours."

She climbed down and removed the ladder. Standing in front of me with a sneer, she hatefully asked. "Would you like a drink of water?"

It pained me to admit it, but of course I did. "Yes."

"Why should I give you any? All you'll do is piss your pants."

And with that, Wilma Huckabee stormed towards her hut, cackling with hurtful glee. I hoped to confirm my earlier sighting of another human inside that structure, but apparently whoever it was had been sufficiently reprimanded for their previous mistake.

How was this for a fine crock of shit? Do you think the possibility of such a scenario was on my mind when I bailed from that Grumman? Hell, no. My fear was that the island would be swarming with Japanese. My hope was to see either friendly humans or no humans at all, but the irony of this, the absurdity of the situation into which I had descended nearly caused me to explode. And the worst of it? The fact that darling Wilma was using religion to manipulate these backwards people to her own devices.

From the first night after my return from mission number one, my first takeoff in attack mode from the deck of the USS Enterprise, my nightmares were of horrible places, of Japanese death marches and camps for prisoners of war. My visions put me into different scenarios of torture, all in which I was stripped naked and unable to move while some cruel interrogator mutilated my body with an endless array of methodical beatings and carvings. Now, here I was in the exact predicament of my dread - naked, stretched, bound and completely at the mercy of a sadist, but not a warrior like me. No, my nightmare-come-true was to be at the hands of a maniacal female and her brainwashed followers. This was not at all an honorable fate for a Navy fighter pilot. This injustice fueled both my anger and my defiance.

How dare she treat me this way. Didn't she know how many times I'd put my life on the line for her? For all Americans? For all of our Allied friends and their countrymen? If she insisted I be her prisoner, fine. Tie me up somewhere, feed me, give me drink, and let me be. But to torture me? Push me to my limits of endurance? Deprive me of the necessities to sustain my life? Who in the fuck did this bitch think she was?

This train of thought did nothing to hurt her, but it was hurting me. My heart raced, blood pressure elevated, sweat glands opened. My body didn't need this. These thoughts only further stressed my already stressed organs, and so I abandoned them.

My little conversation with Wilma Huckabee was somewhat of a relief. Granted, I was still a prisoner, but at least the reason for it was a bit more logical, something I could understand. It also set my mind to searching for various plans of escape or methods of out-thinking her, but I was not given much time for this. The females of the tribe began traipsing into the village carrying baskets full of leaves and branches taken from the forest, which they dumped onto the burning embers of the campfire. Other items, mostly what I guessed to be berries of different colors and nuts of different sizes, were emptied onto the stone slab altar and sorted into wooden bowls, soon to be crushed with rocks and sticks.

An acrid smoke drifted from the now blazing campfire. This burned my overworked nostrils, parched throat and weary eyes, but the pygmies seemed to have grown accustomed to the putrid odor and continued to crush their berries. Without a care for my nearby presence, they mixed their bounty together as though they were concocting their next meal.

What did get their attention was a chorus of high-pitched war whoops coming from outside the village perimeter. Pygmy males had returned from a successful hunt. First, several entered with brightly-feathered and lifeless birds, then came two more triumphantly toting an equally dead boar. All were placed on the altar and the women began to pluck feathers from fowl and fur from pig. A flurry of activity surrounded the area, as the men constructed a wooden spit over the flame, impaling birds to turn and roast one by one as each carcass was prepared. Feathers were saved in bowls and divided by color, while boar hide and its fur was cut into wide strips, then dropped into the same baskets that had been used to gather plants. After its hide was removed, the succulent pig was also impaled for roasting over the fire.

In a way, I was fascinated and just a bit awed by the simple efficiency of these people. Now that I knew the true reason for my suffering, I saw the pygmies as innocents in this tragedy, a once harmless and self-sufficient tribe now corrupted by the she-devil, Wilma Huckabee, who herself was corrupted   by a mindless obsession for those black pearls. And what monetary benefit could she possibly gain from those jewels in this lost world? Nothing. Not that I could see, but I was determined to find out.

She emerged from the church hut, once again adorned in her sanctimonious robe. Like zombies, the congregation stopped what they were doing and followed her to the make-shift scene of my crucifixion, where they silently waited for the next ceremony to begin.

"Children, do you remember the story of the martyrs?"

"Yes, Doctor Wilma."

"And what happened to our brother, Saint Sebastian?"

"Arrows."

"That is correct. Now, we will test this man's faith in the lord. He claims to know Jesus, but does he truly believe? Boban, you and your men climb the trees. Whoever strikes Sebastian from the greatest distance will dine with Doctor Wilma tonight."

I surmised that dining with the doctor was meant to be some sort of special honor, but I couldn't imagine the dinner conversation being anything pleasant.

Each man took one dart from the altar and scattered with blowguns in hand, while the women returned to their food preparations, clearing a path for target practice. As for my antagonist, she stood before me and looked up with an evil grin.

"Should I stop them?"

"I don't know. Are you trying to kill me or make me talk?"

"Oh, don't worry, the arrows are dry. I wouldn't let them poison you before I break you. This is the first time I've had the pleasure of torturing such a strong, handsome man such as yourself. I am so looking forward to seeing you strain those big muscles. Is there anything you'd like to tell me or should we get started?"

"I've already said it."

"Very well." Her eyes moved down to my undershorts, then she smiled and looked into my eyes. "It appears that I am not the only one looking forward to this, Mr. Mitchell. You seem to be growing."

With fingers and thumbs clasped to my waistband she yanked my briefs down to my thighs, completing my nakedness for all to see, and much to my amazement Wilma Huckabee was correct. My penis gallantly sprang from its imprisonment with a dramatic protruding forward – a nearly full-erection state of excitement produced without my help.

The curiosity of this phenomenon matched the humiliation that came with it. My brain could not be responsible for my excitement. Could it? Surely it was a physiological response. Wasn't it? It had to be a result of my suspended bondage and the labored breathing it caused. My brain was deprived of oxygen. My heart was working harder to circulate oxygen throughout my bloodstream, thus sending more blood to my penis than was necessary. This had to be the answer, for the alternative was too horrid to consider. Wilma Huckabee would not be considered regardless the allure of her outer shell. Wilma Huckabee's true self – a woman insane, a woman consumed with greed and sadistic treachery – couldn't possibly be seen as attractive by a man in my predicament, a man subjected to her tortures for no good reason other than to satisfy her insatiable lust to punish him. I refused to allow it.

I dared not comment on my mysterious arousal, but Wilma Huckabee played on her perception that she indeed was the cause. She shredded my briefs with dagger, allowing them to fall to the ground below my feet. She reached with both hands to my chest, planting her palms onto my furred and sweaty skin. She leaned forward and kissed my belly, her sheer robe and the breasts beneath it pressing against the head of my cock. And she taunted me with her words, whispered for my ears only.

"Your manly tool matches your manly physique, Captain Mitchell." Her hands slowly ran the width of my chest side to side, her fingertips lightly scraping my stretched tits. "There's nothing more glorious than a naked man drenched in sweat, crucified, stretched wide open and at my mercy." She tasted her fingers, licked my salt from them. She dug her wet tongue into the depths of my belly button, tasting me there, too. "Defy me for as long as you want. Please, Captain, I beg you. I will enjoy testing your strength. I will take you to your limits of endurance... pain for you... pleasure for me."

She stepped away to reveal my penis fully erect. Her glare upon my tool, her sadistically upturned lips with tongue wetting the upper, as well as her quick hand to her hidden vagina, feigned as a scratch but more of an erotic rub, indicated to me that she liked what she saw. Step by step and piece by piece had Wilma Huckabee dismantled me. My final article of clothing lay at my feet; my nakedness whole; my degradation complete, but if her goal was to defeat me with fear she was on the wrong path, for she unknowingly had provided me with a weapon. I saw her reaction. It was brief but unmistakable. My fully-charged penis, its length and thickness that of a man of her race, man of her size, a length and thickness perhaps greater than she had ever known when she – if she had ever – been in the presence of a normal-height Caucasian male, affected her. I would remember. I would exploit her weakness, beginning right now.

Using only my arms, I lifted myself to breathe. I flexed biceps and triceps, belly, thighs, calves and even feet, arching back my toes. Thrusting forward my chest, I forced it to expand, filling my lungs with air. My lower jaw I forced out, corners of my mouth turned downwards. I looked left and right, admiring my chest with a deep-throated, masculine groan, animal-like, caveman-like.

I displayed myself for her – the naked human male in all his glory, bound in suspension, crucified, and with his magnificent penis fully erect and pointing forward. With a clinching of my scrotum I waved to her, my phallus springing upwards and falling to horizontal again and again as though a giant worm of bait. He spit at her. My obedient cock oozed pre-come. My dangling bait flung my syrup towards her. Soon she would succumb to the epitome of manliness – me.

Brother and sisters, I was gravely mistaken. She scoffed at me. Wilma Huckabee pitched back her head with a sarcastic sneer, and then this she-devil sauntered towards the altar while humming a familiar melody – Onward Christian Soldiers. She could not have done worse had she severed my cock and slapped me in the face with it.

My efforts were not completely in vain, however. To my right, the pygmy women were staring at my air-piercing phallus. Some were in awe, others intimidated. Some giggled, some recoiled, but for good or bad, my antics at the very least captured their attention.

Whatever they were thinking became moot when with a wave of her hand, Wilma commanded to Boban, "You may begin."

The first dart missed me completely, striking the tree trunk inches below my left wrist. Its length extended out of the wood about four inches. Smartly, the pygmies had all climbed different trees and were completely hidden, so I could not see from what direction the next would come. It came from my right, burying itself into my lower abdomen just above my pelvic bone with the same length exposed from me as from the tree trunk. Actually, they were beautiful, these deadly little darts. Shafts made of wood, their back ends were decorated with neatly trimmed and aligned bird feathers, colored black, white, blue, yellow or blood red, colors ironic because red blood began to trickle from the point of my impalement. A small tributary oozed from my puncture wound and trailed hidden through pubic hair before emerging on my right thigh.

The pain itself was nothing more than when our Navy physician administered my annual vaccinations, except that this needle stick continued without interruption.

Another tiny missile followed and this one buried itself deep, striking the center of my left thigh to cause a greater flow of blood and much more pain. I stopped looking. I had no defense, no chance to even flinch, not that it would have lessened the impact had I done so. Instead, I focused on the person who was causing this. The cleverly devious Wilma Huckabee had once again schemed a new, innovative way of twisting religion to her advantage. My naked body's piercing was intended as interrogation for me, while symbolizing a ceremony of faith for the pygmies. After another dart found the center of my arm pit, she halted the proceedings and approached to turn the screws on me a bit.

"How do you feel, Mr. Mitchell?"

"Like I... want to strangle somebody."

"That will change." She scrutinized my form top to bottom, then continued in her charming, southern drawl. "It is a pity to tarnish such a fine, masculine specimen. My, my, I do believe you look good enough to eat."

Again I flexed, partly as a way to defy her, but mostly because I needed to lift myself for oxygen.

"You want to eat, I want to puke."

After a genuine chuckle she softened her tone even more. "That's your fault. Why don't you stop being so silly and tell the truth? I can't bear to watch you suffer like this."

Thus, her reason for exposing her naked body to me earlier – she was tempting me with that robe, knowing full-well that I remembered what was underneath. At the same time, I was tempting her with what she herself had unleashed. My body, my cock in full view, her body, her known to me tits and vagina now covered, were on a collision course. I don't know what she did to suppress her emotions. As for me, all I had to do was gaze upon that red cross embroidered to the center of her robe. Desire turned to hatred. My problem solved.

"Bullshit, you phony bitch," I emphasized what I felt. "You love it or you wouldn't do it."

"Fine," her revealing scowl returned. "Just go ahead and suffer. See if I care."

After she exited the range of fire, I mentally prepared for the next round of arrows by remembering Saint Sebastian himself. The story, in my analysis, is an absurd fairy tale mainly because the time elements are flawed. As an arrow buried itself into the center of my stomach, I closed my eyes.

Sebastian was supposedly enlisted in the Roman Army of the Eastern Empire, soon to be made captain of the Praetorian Guard around A.D. 285 by Diocletian. This Emperor did not know that Sebastian was a Christian, but was curious as to why his captain was so kind to Christian prisoners scheduled to be put to death. So, as punishment for not properly performing these duties of persecution, Diocletian ordered that Sebastian be impaled with arrows, which is what another pygmy version had just done to the tricep of my right arm.

This one jolted me from my contemplation. My eyes opened. My head lowered, chin rested on my chest. The first item I saw was my penis still fully erect and this struck me with a sudden realization. My entire body shuddered at the thought of it. What if these vile pygmies sent one of their darts into my most precious tool? What damage would such a foul deed cause? Permanent? I hoped they were not skilled enough to target me there, which was a ridiculously false hope. Their very survival depended upon the game won by their blow dart talents, so rather than hope they'd miss I prayed instead for their compassion to spare me here regardless of wishes of the white witch. After all, surely there are certain taboos that transcend cultural differences – mutual understandings amongst men that certain deeds are unspeakable, unforgivable. Sadly, hope is all I had. Just the same as with the rest of me, my penis was at their mercy, and so I raised my torso to breathe before throwing back my head, closing my eyes and returning to ancient Rome. Before I got there another arrow found its way into my pectoral muscle, just missing my left nipple.

Sebastian survived his torture of arrows, and then preached to Diocletian about the virtues of this new faith. Big mistake, because hearing this prompted the Emperor's command that Sebastian be beaten to death with fists. That punishment finished him and this is how he became a Christian martyr and saint. The problem with the story is this: Diocletian did not issue his edict to persecute Christians throughout the Empire until 303 – nearly 20 years after this martyrdom supposedly took place. And so, even though it makes for a dramatic yarn the story of Sebastian is just another tool used as a way to keep the sheep believing in something they can't see and can't prove. All they can do is have faith, but to me, a faith should be strong enough to stand on its own words without myths being added years later as reinforcement. Still, the way most of those martyrs died was rather erotic, and great inspiration for artists to reconstruct scenes of muscular men stripped to loin cloth and tortured to death. According to Jesus, though, if you truly believe then you'd never find yourself in such a predic…

A blow dart buried deep into your belly tends to stir your brain from drifting too deeply. I opened my eyes to confirm the latest, a red-black-white feather protruding to the right of my navel midway between navel and pelvic bone. Below that, my phallus was unscathed, still majestically piercing the air. Sebastian was quite a man, you know, standing up to ungodly torture, surviving it and defying his tormentor with speeches of faith. Come to think of it, I'm one hell of a man myself. How long have they tortured me? Not once have I cried out or begged to be released. No, I've shown them how a real man takes punishment. After all, that's what I am. I am one tough son of a bitch. Look at that beautiful man-cock. Damned thing's bigger than anything these little pipsqueaks have ever seen. And come hell or high water, that god damned white witch is gonna feel it... up her ass... down her throat... and oh, yeah... into her gut... Fucking he-man... that's what I am. Think I'll lift myself up... let 'em see what a man can do... torture me, will ya? Crucify me? Like I give a shit... you can't hurt me... I'm more man than you can deal with... I'm more...

Wilma Huckabee lied to me about the pygmy darts. I looked to her for an explanation, but she was not there. My bloodstream raged with testosterone, while my brain put me into the role of a manly, tortured hero. Of course, playing the torture part was easy to do. The pain from suspension and pointed darts was very real, but as for the manly part, those pygmy weapons of impalement undoubtedly assisted me with my performance.

I strained my arms, sucked in my belly, arched my spine and thrust out my chest, displaying my body in all its masculine glory. Females were overwhelmed by this and they abandoned their duties to gather at my feet. The sight of them should have repulsed me – what with their oversized heads and disproportionately long, tubular breasts hanging limp with nipples nearly touching their pelvic bones – but instead, I was further stimulated, especially when I spotted one female whose breasts were perfectly sized for her body, fully plump and rounded, as though begging to be licked. If only I could reach them.

Garbled, high-pitched voices chattered and moaned from all directions, as pygmy males joined the females to rub my legs and feet with rough and tiny hands. Their presence also should have sickened me, but the opposite occurred. My very being raged with lust and the pygmy males enticed me on a level equal to pygmy females. The physiques of these mighty warriors deserved my admiration. Each body was chiseled with masculine beauty, chests and bellies well-defined with muscular lines and curves, plus thick and powerful thighs, calves and arms built for climbing and for speed of foot. A buzz of ultimate rainforest lords clamored around me and I longed to tear away the loin cloth from each one, just to see if their manly tools were pygmy-sized or man-sized.

Climbing ladders, they removed all arrows one by one, and then fondled my chest, arms, face and abdomen. Both males and females engulfed my body from head to toe, not only with hands, but also with lips and tongues. The trails of blood were licked from my skin, while lubricated palms and fingers coated my penis and testicles with a thick, greasy liquid. It burned – a maddening, feverish stimulation. All hands were laid upon me. Pygmy fingers, palms and nails spread the oil to every surface of my skin. Previously unresponsive areas of me became first-time erogenous zones. Erogenous zones became heightened triggers of animalistic lust. Their mesmerizing touch lavished the erotic oil into my hair, onto my face, into my arm pits, onto my chest and belly, into the skin between my fingers and toes, onto my feet and hands and thighs and shins and calves and pubic hair and testicles and penis, and I writhed with ecstasy. My torso thrust forward as though performing a vertical swan dive. No more the pain of suspension; no more the agony of crucifixion; no more struggling for air; no more hunger; no more thirst, I sacrificed myself to them, pygmy men and pygmy women, my body basking in their incredible worship, my senses consumed with my own masculinity.

Hank Mitchell was the manliest man in the entire universe and I told them so with grunts and groans, with muscular flexing, thrusting and posing. I physically begged them to lavish me with their praise. Every pygmy hand granted my wish. Every pygmy mouth kissed and licked in a frenzied blur of maddening stimulation. My tantalizing admirers became a black coating of jiggled pudding, a squirming layer of nondescript worms – except for one. She of the rounded breasts was no blur to me. She of natural, savage beauty stood out clearly, positioned directly before my penis. She of my secret desires – desires never before entertained or even known before my lustful eyes locked onto her gorgeous breasts, her woman-sized tits attached to pygmy-sized form – this is the female who opened her jaws to maximum diameter and engulfed my penis. She sucked out my manly seed. She swallowed it, caught her breath, and came back for more.

Two times did she drain me of my fluids, and then, she approvingly selected others to also taste. Some used their mouths. Some combined oil with hands. Both methods effectively milked me time and again. My stamina never wavering, my lust never subsiding, I continued to writhe, flex and display myself for them. I desired their touch. They demanded my seed. And each of us every one was satisfied. My interaction with the pygmies continued for hours until their bellies were filled and my semen drained. They left me hanging, my exhausted body collapsing into full suspension. Too weak to writhe, too weak to flex, nearly too weak to breathe, my chin rested on my chest with every muscle relaxed. There was serenity, peace, a sense of victory, but still my phallus projected forward fully charged and prepared for battle.

Fantasy? Probably. But what did it matter? In my memory all was real regardless of physical impossibilities. The pygmies gave to me an ecstasy beyond words, internally with their darts, externally with their oil, hands, lips and tongues. Besides, nobody knows what miracles the body human can perform unless it is required to do so. My insatiable lust remained strong even as I was released from my crucifixion bondage.

They cut my binding ropes and cradled me. I was carried triumphantly towards the stream – not in the painful manner of the earlier procession, but horizontally and face down as they lovingly supported me in their many arms. Once there, they turned me onto my back and repeatedly submerged my body to cleanse it, which allowed me to quench my ungodly thirst. I was taken below the water's surface but for a few seconds, and then above it for several more. With a ritualized and repetitive dunking, a sort of baptism perhaps, the pygmies comforted me in their cool-water stream, all the while moaning and chanting in a language not English but all their own.

The stimulating oil washed away, and with its disappearance my pain returned. My tortured body was massaged, my muscles and joints deep-rubbed, as my pygmy admirers restored me in their cool water. With the oil no longer saturating my skin, my heightened lust also subsided, but the internal stimulant continued to heat my blood with testosterone. My elevated sense of manliness remained strong, my penis strong, my sense of reality fogged.

Light was fading and so was I. The incessant chatter of their tribal language became distant. Their meat-tenderizing fingers and hands cast me into complete collapse, my mind drifting far from their comforting stream. And yet, whether a dream or a reality, my attention was given to a blurred line at stream's edge. It appeared as another procession, perhaps humans, perhaps something else. My vision could not be focused to determine which. The line was moving away from the stream and towards the village. A ghostly figure floated amongst the dark mass, towering above and leading it further into the distance, and as it blurred to nothingness, a human voice shouted. The words were mostly garbled and the tone was of anger, but one single-syllable sound came through loud and clear – steak... or stake – same sound, different meanings. How could I have cared one way or another?

After another pygmy-controlled dunking and resurfacing, the forms in the fog were gone, as was my consciousness. Finally, my marathon day of torture and suffering and ejaculation and ecstasy was ended. Both my mind and my body drifted far from my island of capture and I rested in darkness.

The Gift of Gamay

Lay down all thoughts, surrender to the void, it is shining…

John Lennon was five years old when the pygmies were dunking me in their stream, but these lyrics he wrote 20 years later aptly describe where my state of mind needed and wanted to go.

I needed guidance, however, to help me get there. So many questions, such a long list that I did not know where to begin, had to be put aside for now. It was done with the help of voices, some recognized and others not. Guardian angels? Could be, but one clearly understood came directly from the database called my brain, my memories of Uncle John.

The gist of his advice? *Try not to try too hard.* The first time he told me this was on one of those fateful Sundays. He'd stopped by in his Jenny to take me on a recreational flight above Ogle County – a gift from John to me on my 13th birthday. Surely, the importance of this far outweighed the meaningless drivel of Sunday church, or so I thought. My dad, John's brother, thought otherwise and my mother agreed with him wholeheartedly. My reaction was very unchurch-like, spiked with profanity and dramatized by stomping and kicking and snorting worthy of a spoiled brat, which I normally was not.

Of course, punishment had to follow. I was forbidden to go anywhere other than school, home and (have mercy, lord) church for one solid month. Poor Uncle John could not save me from any of it, could not go against the commands of his brother and sister-in-law, but he could comfort me with hope. He could offer me words of advice, as I swore to him privately that come hell or high water I was getting out of Adeline two seconds after my high school graduation. He could agree with me that yes, I should and would do exactly that, but for now, "Bide your time," he told me. "Some things can't be fixed no matter how hard you try, son. Plant a seed and let it grow awhile, then it'll spring up to hit you like a hammer. Wait for it, Hank. You'll know."

Who could have predicted that a tyrant of pure evil named Adolph Hitler would be that hammer? Join the Air Force. Learn to fly, learn to fight like Uncle John did in the war to end all wars. See the world, maybe even help save it. On October 23, 1941, my 18th birthday, I signed my commitment to join them upon completion of my high school graduation. On December 08 of that year I changed my enlistment to the United States Navy for the obvious reasons of revenge, and the week before Christmas my education began – Great Lakes Naval Station Training Facility, boot camp. Goodbye, Adeline. I'm leaving five months ahead of schedule.

From out of the sky I had fallen into the grips of a different sort of tyrant, one Wilma Huckabee. From the clutches of evil, from the agonies of torture I was taken to the waters of baptism and comfort. Here I remained, allowing the hallucinogen to lead me wherever it wanted me to go. Submerged beneath the moonlit water's surface, floating in total surrender, I was released from fear and pain. Insight replaced my hatred. My savior had come – not in the form of some obscure, hypothetical deity, but as a woman. I sensed an all-knowing presence hovering close to me, an entity of intelligence, a guide to erase my confusion, a power to restore my strength.

A gentle hand supporting my head and wooden bowl pressing my lips lifted me above the unfocused line, the division between fog and clarity.

"Drink, Mitchell... drink."

Kneeling beside my chest was a true queen of the pygmies, she of the rounded breasts. Her ebony skin shimmered in soft light, her black hair hinted of dark purple and was closely cropped but fluffed and following the contours of her over-sized skull.

I sipped and swallowed. A thick, milky substance with the flavor of bitter chocolate jolted my senses, but was welcomed because it enabled my eyes to once again focus. After emptying the bowl, I inspected my surroundings – the inside of a hut, dimly lit by a low-flamed torch stuck into the dirt near the center space. A large mat made from dried and woven strips of foliage served as flooring, while lined neatly in rows near one wall were wooden utensils and tools. A small cross made of wood stood upright near the torch and this completed the inside contents of the living quarters.

Me? Naked, wrists and ankles wrapped with vine-woven ropes, ropes tied to wooden stakes, stakes driven through the mat and into the dirt, my body was spread eagle and stretched taut, but not to the point of any great discomfort. Upon each of my darted puncture wounds was smeared a white paste which had not only stopped the blood flow, but also numbed my skin at the areas of piercing. My skin was washed of all sweat and dirt. I could feel it, smell it.

"Now, you eat." She released the back of my head, discarded the drinking bowl and retrieved another, taking from it a chunk of cooked and still-warm meat. "Eat, Mitchell," as she dangled the aromatic strip above my lips.

Famished, I clenched it between my teeth and nearly swallowed it whole, and then another was offered. I took it, but this time chewed and savored and spoke to her. "Boar meat?"

Her response was to frown with a look of puzzlement, so I tried again.

"Pig?"

"Yes, pig... pig for Mitchell."

"What is your name?"

"Name?" She pointed to herself and I nodded yes. "Gamay." She covered her mouth with her hand and giggled as though a bashful school girl, and then she placed a finger in front of her lips. "Talk quiet, Mitchell."

"I will talk quiet, Gamay," I whispered and I smiled. "Thank you for my food... and my drink."

I continued to engulf each chunk of succulent meat as it was offered, speaking to her with mouth full. "This is your home? Where you live?"

"Yes."

"You are alone? In this home?"

"No. I belong to Boban."

"Did Boban kill pig? For you?

"Yes. He kills for all."

"Who makes darts... arrows... to kill pig?"

"Boban and men."

"And men make medicine... for darts?"

She did not understand this.

"Medicine... drug... liquid... on dart... to kill pig."

Her eyes brightened. "Men make darts. Women make mix."

"To kill pig."

She nodded, and then giggled. "I make mix so Mitchell happy." And then, Gamay sat down my bowl. On all fours, she straddled my chest and hovered with her face directly above mine. "I make mix for Mitchell not to hurt. I make mix for us... mix from baskets, mix in bowls... we eat mix, too, Boban and men, Gamay and women."

"And the white woman?"

"No, not white woman... us. Doctor Wilma not see. We eat. I make us like you... with mix."

A more accurate description would be to say she made us all *horny* with mix, had she known what the word meant.

This was my savior, a pharmaceutical wizard who'd taken pity on me. Unbeknownst to Wilma Huckabee, Gamay cleverly numbed my pain with the very darts intended to torture me. But how had Gamay kept our frenzied orgy a secret from the white witch? How had our melee escaped her notice?

These questions would have to wait, because Gamay no longer listened. She talked. Gamay became a ceaseless fountain of information. She fed me, gave me drink and proudly told of her people without my asking. Gamay's English was elementary but easily understood, and her story was invaluable to me. Men of her tribe were the hunters and builders, using stones to sharpen bones for daggers and daggers to sharpen wood for darts. The women were experts at mixing potions from plants and amphibians. They knew how to make every kind of mix from the natural surroundings in their rainforest home, knowledge handed down from one generation to the next. They'd learned to make poisons for hunting game, drugs and pastes for alleviating pain, healing of infections and healing of flesh wounds. With their mixes they also produced tranquilizers, aphrodisiacs and hallucinogens, which once had been used for ritualistic ceremonies, one of which was revived for me.

And the pre-Christian name of this tribe? Balingiga. But now, thanks to the western intruder, they called themselves pygmies. Their leader? Boban, who by birthright was their chieftain, but was now just a lackey, usurped of his powers by Wilma Huckabee.

Everything they needed was provided for them by their rainforest home, including the fresh-water stream. As Gamay told her tale, her eyes scrutinized my naked form, drifting from my chest to my toes with a look of intrigue and lust – not drug-induced, but very genuine, and when her story was ended, when my feeding was complete, Gamay expressed what she was thinking. "Strong man, Mitchell."

I seized upon this, straining my arms to expand my chest and flex for her. "Will you touch?"

She gingerly, almost timidly placed fingers onto my stomach, and then began to rub with her palms. She kneaded my abdominal muscles with her tiny digits and let out a slight moan of admiration. "Strong."

"Gamay, I must urinate." It was true. I was desperate.

She removed her hands and looked to me with puzzlement. "Your-e-nate?"

"I must evacuate... piss... pee..."

"Pee!"

"Yes, I need to pee!"

She ran to the wall and picked out a bowl, returning with it to delicately lift my penis and drape it over the bowl's rim. "Pee, Mitchell."

I expanded my chest, sucked in my belly and thrust upward my pelvis, and with a deep-toned and masculine groan of satisfaction I filled her bowl.

When the stream subsided to droplets, she kindly asked, "Pee gone?"

"Not all. You make gone."

She gently encircled my peter in the palm of her hand, then squeezed with fingers to milk it dry.

"Mmm, Gamay pretty." I stretched and posed, inviting her to continue handling my organ while I gathered more information. "Where is Boban?"

"With doctor Wilma. His dart best. They eat." She set aside the urine bowl and switched to squeeze my tool in the fist of her right hand while confidently massaging my chest and belly with her open-palmed left. "I fix you, Mitchell, look."

Using her index finger, she removed the salve from each of my puncture wounds one by one, and miraculously, the holes were barely visible.

"How did you do it, Gamay?"

"Secret," she whispered. "I fix strong man."

"Mmm, you are good. Fix me more."

With my bladder empty, I now could concentrate on becoming aroused by her touch, but at the same time continue the questioning.

"Will Boban come here?"

"Yes. He watches you."

"Will he sleep?"

"No. He watches you."

"You will make him sleep. Yes?"

Before she could answer, I clinched my scrotum and caused my fully-erect organ to surge in her hand. Gamay hesitated, momentarily startled, but soon she progressed from squeezing my cock in her fist to stroking him in her gentle hand. Gamay flashed her teeth, fascinated and excited and tempted. "For Mitchell, Boban will sleep."

"Mmm, I like Gamay. We wait," I enticed while arching my back and flattening my belly to further woo her. "I will sleep. You fix me when Boban sleeps."

Gamay was the perfect caretaker for Mitchell. She followed my instructions flawlessly, and although I don't know how long she allowed me sleep, I was stirred awake by her hand once again squeezing me. Past her and to my right, Boban laid on his side facing us, his eyes closed in a peaceful slumber. I trusted Gamay. I did not ask her if she had put him out with one of her concoctions, for I knew that indeed she had and was now fearless in her desire to service me.

The torchlight was quickly fading and in near-darkness she gently stroked my organ with the rough and tiny fingers of her right hand. Kneeling beside me, she involved her left hand with deep rubs to my chest and belly.

Make no mistake, I needed Gamay. I needed at least one member of the Balingiga tribe to be on my side, or at least be curious enough to defend me from harm and provide me with information. But other elements were involved here. I longed for this female and my desire was pure. No aphrodisiacs persuaded me, no drugs elevated my want. My mind was clear, my lust very real. I was staked to the dirt floor of her home, my arms and legs spread wide, my chest, belly and penis vulnerable to her touch. A beautiful woman of ebony skin – the size of a girl but with features of a buxom female – completely controlled me. The heat stifled, air heavy and wet. The atmosphere of ancient civilization, when nakedness meant beauty, before confining rules and morals were invented to suppress expressions of mutual admiration between man and woman, brought to me new and exciting sensations and the freedom to unleash them. Gamay and I were wildly attracted, focused and ready to explore, and my female partner would do with me as she pleased.

Juices of excitement trickled from underneath her loin cloth and down her inner thighs, as she explored my Caucasian form, features of a man unlike any in her Balingiga tribe. My body hair fascinated her. She hand-rubbed my belly, lifting tufts of belly hair between her fingers and thumbs. She tugged on them; with her index fingers she made swirls of them, the wetness of my sweat acting as paste to hold her designs in place. She leaned down to redesign her work by using her tongue, tasting my sweat, tugging my belly hairs with her lips.

Gamay followed my line of fur above my navel and along the center of my stomach, again tugging with first her fingers and then her lips. With her right hand she cupped my testicles, and there too did she tug on male hair while at the same time pressing her face into my stomach and fiddling with her left-hand the hairs on my chest.

After removing her hands and face from me, Gamay silently inspected with her eyes. She glared at my chest, specifically my stretched wide open nipples. Her men had nothing of the like – theirs are flat, large circles; mine are small dots. Balingiga tips are level with their rims; mine are raised and pointed. Gamay reached down to touch mine, exploring, experimenting. Her rough little fingers rubbed my tips. Her fingers and thumbs lightly pinched and twisted, and I bolted. My back arched to the maximum my bindings would allow. A previously unknown sense of masculinity consumed me, as once again, just as with her mix Gamay unleashed testosterone to rage throughout my insides.

Yes, I was tortured by this woman, but it was not her intent. Besides, this was a torture no man could refuse. So small and inferior she was, yet Gamay was in complete control of me, so I lingered. She forced me to linger so she could explore every inch of me, and I relished it. I writhed with ecstasy as she licked and sucked my tits. I breathed heavily as her tongue traversed the length of my body. She removed my sweat, painted me with her spit. She kissed and licked my bound hands, sucked on my fingers. She saturated my bushy-haired arm pits, darkened my dark chest hairs. She filled my belly button with her saliva, then squished it out with her tongue. She gnawed at my legs with wet lips, coating my right thigh, knee and shin with her spit. She worked my feet same as my hands, wetting my arches, sucking my toes. And with a return trip the length of my left shin, left knee, left thigh, Gamay's courage, Gamay's desire brought her to lay atop me. She valiantly maneuvered my rock-hard cock beneath her loin cloth. My corona felt her wetness, as she positioned her vagina to make contact. Her knees straddled my hips. Her heavenly breasts fit perfectly into my flattened, downward-sloping stomach. She gathered her strength and forced my penis inside her – one inch, and then another, and then another, and then she waited.

Had she gone too far? Would my length and girth cause her pain? Damage?

Gamay was in control. She would decide. I was in ecstasy. She could do as she pleased.

More of my cock was taken, and then she gave some of it back. Laying flat atop me, Gamay targeted herself – my giant mushroom to her tiny clit. She rubbed herself slowly to and fro, and with each contact of my corona to her baby dick the pressure in my nuts intensified. Gamay took me deeper, little by little, each of her undulations thoroughly stimulating both of us – on the fore stroke, on the back stroke, and in silence she took us nearer to mutual explosion. She sensed my coming; I sensed hers. And as my back arched and chest expanded for release, this glorious woman reached up with both hands to pinch my tits while frantically rubbing hers on my sweat-drenched stomach.

It took great effort for Gamay and I to express our pleasure in silence. Tiny grunts and moans did slip out, but all drama was confined to our loins. We mated, this woman and I, our orgasms simultaneous, and although I longed to hold her in my arms for our comedown, to smother

her ebony-skinned breasts, nose, lips and tongue with my kisses, all was good. Gamay was in control. She knew what she was doing and was pleased with her discovery. "Mr. Simon weak in Gamay... Mitchell strong."

"Huh?"

Exploiting the Babes

I bit my tongue, saved my question. Our afterglow was too perfect for verbal interruption, and besides, I certainly wasn't going anywhere and neither was Gamay. Neither of us moved. She laid atop me, straddling, her breasts crushing into my stomach, cheek resting on my chest and fingers twirling its hairs as she kept us connected, allowing my penis to deflate inside her. And we listened to one another breathe.

To my right and to her left, Boban's sleeping continued as before, his position unchanged. Her sacrifice to me – the risks she'd taken, the pleasures she'd given, demanded my appreciation and I strained my neck with an attempted kiss to the top of Gamay's head, but she was out of reach so I softly spoke. "Thank you, Gamay."

Shifting herself towards me, Gamay allowed my flaccid penis to slip out of her, and then laid flat to press her breasts firmly close to mine while rubbing her loin cloth along the length of my belly. "Mitchell happy?"

"Yes, Gamay." Now I could kiss her scalp and did. "Mitchell is happy."

 Gamay happy."

"It is good, Gamay. You like Mitchell more... not Mr. Simon."

"Yes. I like Mitchell."

"Gamay, who is Mr. Simon?"

"He is for doctor Wilma."

"He came with her?"

"They came. She hides him now."

"Can he come to Gamay's home?"

"No, forbidden."

"Why?"

"He stays in church. Tied, like Mitchell."

"Doctor Wilma ties him?"

"She tells Boban. Simon is tied."

Wheels were spinning, as I pressed on. "Gamay, do you see Mr. Simon?"

"No more. Mr. Simon sick in head. Long ago. No Simon, Gamay likes Mitchell."

She pressed her nose into my chest, tasted its skin with her tongue. Weary of talk, Gamay prepared to launch another assault upon my available body, but Mitchell was not strong for her. My spine ached. For hours I'd laid on it, my arms and legs bound and stretched spread eagle. I needed to bend my knees, bend my backbone, and without the drug to assist me, my cock was unresponsive. Worst of all, the rubbing of her rough animal hide loin cloth to my belly soon involved my penis as well. It hurt like hell, soon to be raw and sore. It was my only available weapon and Gamay unknowingly was rendering it useless. Something had to give.

"Gamay, take off your cloth."

Immediately, she sprang up and off of me, then crawled away to kneel in the distance. "Forbidden... only Doctor Wilma says."

In the dark shadow, only one item came into view. It was the white cross painted at the crotch of each female covering, including Gamay's.

"Wilma says who touches Gamay?"

"Cross hides Gamay."

"Does Boban touch?"

"No, forbidden."

Nausea hit the pit of my stomach, as I realized the severity of Wilma Huckabee's control over these people. Not only did it extend to deciding which ones could breed and which ones couldn't, but worse, she also chose who was to breed with whom, which prompted that hammer of which Uncle John spoke to finally whack me between the eyes.

"Gamay, where are the children... babies?"

There was no answer, as she sat with head cast downward.

"Where are small Balingiga... the little ones?"

"Little ones," she hesitated, trying to decide whether or not to answer what should not have been asked. "At church."

"With Doctor Wilma?"

"They belong to church."

"Are they at church now?"

"Night at church. Day at cave."

"What cave?"

"Cave of black rock."

"What is at the cave?"

"Black rock."

I was within seconds of cursing aloud the name of Wilma Huckabee, thus bringing the entire tribe down upon us, but managed to clench my teeth and hold my tongue. This evil woman had not only crossed the line of human decency, but stomped it into the ground. No longer was I concerned with my own predicament because suddenly, my raging obsession, my blind motivation was to stop her by any means necessary. It had to be done. I had to somehow prevent the complete obliteration of the Balingiga before their own memories of their own culture was forgotten and lost forever. This was an unwarranted annihilation of an innocent people brought about by greed, and the battle to be fought inside our little village had become just as important to me as the battle of nations taking place outside of it.

"Gamay, untie me."

"No, Mitchell, forbidden."

"You must. Doctor Wilma is evil."

"No, Mitchell, I will die."

She was correct. The fear instilled was too deeply imbedded to be swept away in one evening, and besides, I had no right to put her into such danger. With my greatest fear being the loss of her admiration and trust, I planted a seed.

"Gamay, I am sorry. I should not ask. Come close."

Timidly, she crawled back to lay her head on my chest, "I am sorry, Mitchell."

"You are good to me, Gamay. I am happy. We are friends. Do not be sorry." Straining to lift my head, I placed a kiss into her fluffed hair. "I want you to go to Boban. Take off his cloth. Fix Boban like you fix Mitchell."

"No, Mitchell. It is bad."

"It is not bad. That is a lie. Boban is Balingiga chief. Gamay is his woman. Fix him."

A female Balingiga tear fell onto my chest, then Gamay lifted her head off of me and reluctantly crawled towards Boban, rolling him onto his back. Musical tones of high-pitched whimpers drifted throughout the hut, as Gamay made love to her semi-conscious warrior. When the first glimmers of morning sun streaked into our nest, its light revealed a woman lying atop a man. Gamay and Boban, locked in a slumbering embrace, were one. With two loin cloths piled in a heap nearby, the penis of Boban was properly inserted, captured and lovingly squeezed by the woman who loved him. Gamay imprisoned her man with vaginal squeezes, and if all my hopes were to come true, never again would she let him go. No huckster-designed, false symbol could possibly prevent what was meant to be.

With memories stirred, seeds planted, I watched and waited, certain that Wilma Huckabee had a busy day planned, but before she could worry about me her number one priority had to be addressed. Far away, in the direction of the church hut, voices of children moaned and grumbled in a manner similar to youngsters who lament the end of summer, children who protest being awakened for the first day of a new school year. To hell with that. It reminded me of myself when I was a disgruntled child being forced out of my bed by my parents on a cold Sunday morning.

The reverent Wilma gathered all in the central clearing and coaxed her child-slave laborers to behave.

"Come, children, sing with me. *Jesus loves me, this I know, for the Bible tells me so.*"

With absolutely no enthusiasm, the chorus joined in, "*Little ones to him belong. They are weak, but he is strong.*"

Oh, god, the sound of it depressed me – angered me. Shysters? Counterfeits? Charlatans? Call them what you will, but that little song has been used by all of them to brainwash the unsuspecting. The lyrics say it all, and certainly I myself nearly fell prey to its manipulative message. Sure, I was forced to sing it many times. It says the Bible tells me so, and therefore it's automatically true, no questions asked. It says I belong to him, which has to be because I am weak and inferior and always will be unless I give myself to him. Easier said than done, considering I can't see him or touch him.

If explained properly and with compassion, that little tune isn't such a bad thing. The problem is that the shysters, counterfeits and charlatans substitute themselves for Jesus. That's how they manipulate. That's how you can always tell they're up to no good. They preach as though they've been to heaven and have come back to tell it all, and if you don't do this or you do do that then you're going the other direction – straight to hell. And once they've got you good and scared, that's when they reach into your pocket and pick you clean. Guilt money – give me 10% of your hard-earned income – buy your ticket to salvation – or else.

Why do parents subject their children to such a frightening experience? How could a child possibly understand the Bible? A book that contradicts itself from one page to the next? How could they comprehend the psycho-babble of any religious philosophy? These words are confusing enough for adults. How could the Balingiga possibly know the dangers of believing that one human being has all the answers?

They couldn't, but let's say for the sake of argument that the true teachings of Jesus Christ are a very real thing. If so, then he surely must have dropped me onto this island to save these people from a treacherous huckster, a con artist named Wilma Huckabee. Jesus could not have selected a better candidate, for this woman was not the first god-spouting counterfeit to bring pain into my life.

The preacher at our church during my early years was a mostly harmless man. Elderly, soft-spoken and humble, his heart was kind and he spoke to us children in the same manner as our teachers at school – slowly, clearly and with word choices we could understand. None of it made sense to me, but at least going to church wasn't such a traumatic event back then.

In my eighth year of life that man retired from his preaching duties. That's when all hell broke loose. The church hierarchy in Chicago sent a man who yelled at us – screamed from the pulpit to everybody in the congregation about the awful things that were going to happen to us. His preaching based on volume, he worked his hour-long drama with a slow-building crescendo until nearly raising the rafters with his diatribes against alcohol and fornication and any other activity for pleasure of which he was against. Fire and eternal damnation – that's what awaited anyone who tried to enjoy life. But of course, his speech always ended softly and with long, drawn-out pauses, as he explained how Jesus died for our sins, and that everything we'd done bad would be forgiven if we accept the fact that he did it all for us – provided that we didn't do it again.

Such a pleasant image for an impressionable young mind – some poor schmuck stripped to his loin cloth and nailed to a giant wooden letter t with blood spewing everywhere – that guy must have really pissed somebody off. With a little research of my own, I discovered that the Romans did that to thousands of bad guys for the same reason we now use the electric chair or a noose, and I wondered how come we never had to pray for all those people, or people of different faiths, or different colors of skin. Doesn't Jesus forgive them for their sins, too? In other words, I started thinking for myself, which usually leads to the collapse of logic when listening to these sermons.

My parents learned. Everybody did, when about seven years later our preacher told the congregation that he'd received a vision. Jesus himself thought we deserved a new church building, and so our preacher drew up the design he said he'd envisioned, figured up the cost estimates to make it happen and started a fund-raising drive to pay for it. And the best part? The church hierarchy would kick in 25% if the congregation could come up with the rest. They did, and for most members it was a burden, but it certainly shook their faith when our preacher got the 25% from Chicago, cashed it, and disappeared with 100% of the money raised.

That was the end of church-going for the Mitchell family. It also made for a very lean Christmas and beyond, and to my knowledge that man has never been captured, but I'm sure my mom and dad would be proud to help me nail him to a cross just the way the Romans did to Jesus and all the others. So, Jesus, you pitiful tortured soul, I'll be more than happy to do your bidding in your little tiff with Dr. Wilma Huckabee.

"Gamay," I whispered as loudly as possible. "Gamay, wake up."

She opened her eyes and slowly lifted off of Boban. His long pole slowly emerged fully erect, until the union of penis and vagina was broken.

"Put on your cloth, and Boban's. Then come close to me."

She ignored the first part and crawled to kneel beside me naked, facing away from me so she could gaze at her still-naked and sleeping Boban.

"Listen. Little ones are singing."

"They go to cave."

"Why does doctor Wilma take only little ones?"

"Only little ones can go."

"Why?"

"They are little."

"Why only little ones for cave?"

"Hole of cave... little."

"Where are black rocks?"

"In little hole... in water... below little hole... in cave."

As the singing voices faded, I began to appreciate the logic of Huckabee's breeding theory. Once children grew to a certain size, they no longer could enter the hole inside cave to dive for her black pearls, and so she matched up only the smallest adults in hopes of creating smaller infants – smaller Balingiga, who could serve her needs for a longer time.

This, of course, made me wonder why she didn't just have the men open up the god damned hole. No matter. She chose her own method and she needed her pygmies to be smaller than pygmies for as long as possible.

By comparison to other males Boban was in the taller range, while Gamay's body was more round and wide than other females, therefore, Boban and Gamay were forbidden intercourse. Based on what I'd seen, I suspected that Wilma Huckabee might soon find it more difficult to prevent Balingiga pokes from taking place, at least between these two. The only mystery remaining about the chief and his woman pertained to how much of the experience Boban would remember what his reaction to it would be.

"Good, Gamay," I reassured her. "Mitchell is happy. You wake Boban. Mitchell will sleep."

And wake him she did, but in an unexpected way. Straddling Boban's hips, she deep massaged his chest and belly until he opened his eyes and sat up in puzzlement.

"Crazy woman... what are you doing?"

"I wake my Boban." She coaxed him to again lie flat, and then resumed her rub.

"You lay quiet."

"You cannot do this," he half-heartedly protested. "It is... forbidden."

Boban stretched his arms past his head and absorbed her praise. He couldn't help himself. Gamay is a very talented female. He never made a move when she grabbed hold of his penis and manipulated it in her hand. Pretending to sleep, I spied an excited phallus, instantly erect from her touch, its expansion spreading apart the fingers of Gamay. Proportional to his body-size Boban was a very healthy male, and within seconds Gamay had his tool comfortably buried into her warm, wet mouth. Can there be any better way for a man to start his day?

Boban closed his eyes, and so did I. The heavenly sounds of his high-pitched but manly grunts soothed my aching back, as I imagined Boban's ecstasy, relived what I myself had felt. The beautiful Gamay drained her man, swallowed him, making certain that he'd been properly awakened.

"Now, Boban," she instructed while handing him his loin cloth. "Watch Mitchell sleep. I get food for us."

As she dutifully grabbed several bowls and left the hut, I stretched in a feigned awakening and turned to look at my guard. Boban sat next to my chest with his legs crossed, penis safely hidden under his loin wrapping and teeth slightly exposed between contented lips.

"Good morning, Boban."

Quickly, he assumed a look of sternness to affirm his authority. "Quiet. You do not talk."

"Gamay is pretty. You are lucky man."

His eyes dreamily stared into space and his face transformed into that of a pubescent boy, "Her lips are good to me."

"All of Gamay is good to you. Even under the cross on her cloth."

Boban's grasp of the English language was much better than Gamay's. He instantly understood my teasing, which caused him to chuckle and puff up his chest with pride. But then he caught himself, remembering that his new discovery should be kept a secret. "I do not know."

"You should know. She is your female."

"No," he shouted and leapt to his feet. "That is for Doctor Wilma."

"Why? Because she says? Think, Boban. It is not right. Gamay is your female. You should say. Not the white woman."

"No. You are evil. I do not listen to you."

And with that he stomped his little foot into my stomach and started to leave the hut, but he couldn't. The wheels were turning in his head. Boban started to think for himself, and so he returned to sit and continue our chat.

"You told her to do it."

"She is Balingiga. You are Balingiga chief. You are her man. That is why she did it."

"She is for Jesus and Doctor Wilma. No more."

"The Balingiga belong to you, Boban. You are their chief, not the white woman."

"She makes miracles."

"What miracles?"

"Doctor Wilma makes fire. Jesus tells her how to do it."

"That is a lie, Boban," I burst into laughter. "Any man can make fire."

"No. *You* lie. Only Doctor Wilma."

"You are wrong. She lies."

"You cannot. You show me. I prove you lie."

After retrieving a dagger, Boban proceeded to cut my bindings beginning with my left ankle, and would have completely freed me had it not been for the commotion coming from the village clearing.

"Forbidden! Sinner! Doctor Wilma, come." The voice was female, an hysterical female.

With mutual expressions of dread, Boban and I looked at one another as the name we feared pierced the air.

"Gamay has sinned... Doctor Wilma, Gamay must be punished!"

Boban stood and again stomped me in the gut. "You are the devil, Mitchell. You will die for what you have done to me."

He turned to leave, but not before I had my say. "You are the chief of your Balingiga people, Boban. Gamay is your woman. You must save her."

"She cannot be saved."

"Then you are no Balingiga warrior. You are slave to the white woman. Boban is not a man."

After hesitating to think on these words, he ran from the hut, abandoning me to wonder whether he would fight for his woman or sacrifice her to the mercy of that counterfeit Christian.

Born Again

My left ankle was free.

With screams, shouts, moans and cries echoing from the village clearing outside, I slid the arch of my left foot under the ankle of my right, and then used the strength of both legs to lift upwards. Success! The stake pinning my right ankle emerged from the dirt and I somersaulted in reverse, rose to my feet, grabbed the two remaining stakes and pulled them up like turnips from the soil. Rummaging through the pygmy tools produced a dull-edged, knife-like eating utensil, which I used to saw on the vine-ropes until one by one I could rip the strands apart with my fingers. Meanwhile, the voice of Wilma Huckabee, who had been summoned from the cave tried to restore calm.

"What has this woman done?"

"She fixed Mr. Simon."

"How?"

The answer must have been given with a physical demonstration, because after a few seconds of silence a gasp was followed by a mighty roar of angry shouts.

Oh, god... what had I wrought? Nothing. Wilma Huckabee did it. She's the one who forced Gamay to suppress what should never be denied, and now that her shackles were broken, poor Gamay had endeavored to make up for years of time lost. Mr. Simon weak... Mitchell strong? Who cares? For Gamay, any dick would do.

With the last vine removed, I slithered on my belly towards the opening of the hut and carefully peeked out. Gamay was standing, stripped naked and held by two men, while the remaining Balingiga gathered around the stone altar.

Positioned between the altar and the church hut with eyes cast downward was Boban, who apparently had made the decision to side with the mob. And next to him, the white-robed Wilma Huckabee was scheming some sort of ritualistic sentence for poor Gamay.

"Brothers and sisters, this is a fallen woman. She has gone astray. She is unclean and must confess her sins. Raise her onto the altar so we can pray for our lost Gamay. Pray for her soul."

Men lifted Gamay to lie face up on the stone slab, and then held down her torso and closed their eyes while the preacher bent forward, placing her hands upon Gamay's prone body. Huckabee prayed; the tribe mimicked; and Boban stood silently outside the circle gathered around the altar.

Showing no fear, his Balingiga queen kept silent and did not struggle for escape, but instead undulated with an ecstatic writhing, the hands of her tribesmen and the white woman only further simulating her. Years of sexual frustration, of suppressed yearning had been set free. Once an obedient zombie, Gamay now was a glorious, sensitive, expressionistic vessel of human beauty and want – just as she was born to be – just as we all are born to be. If the charlatan Christian's intent was to force the heavenly Gamay back into that cocoon, she was in for a big surprise. I could not allow it. My love queen had to be rescued.

Silently, I crawled from the hut, moved behind it and out of view, then bolted into the covering of the rainforest. Sneaking from the rear of one structure to another, I made my way to the backside of the church hut, where I proceeded to tear open a hole and find the man called Mr.

Simon.

He was seated on the ground with his legs flat. Using his fingers, he calmly shoveled food from a wooden bowl to his mouth. He sat naked, his skin milky-white, his age 20 years beyond my own and maybe more. His ankles were wrapped in ropes of vine with a connecting rope of enough length to allow him shuffling, but not walking. His body was gaunt and frail either from lack of nourishment or exercise or both, and after glancing up for a few seconds with a blank stare he returned to his meal as though nothing else was of importance – neither I nor my intrusion nor the hubbub outside his hut.

At the altar, sanctimonious sobbing, moaning and praying droned on unabated as I addressed this peculiar man. "Are you Simon?"

"Yes," he stopped eating long enough to answer. "I am... Simon... I am... Simon Huckabee."

"Do you know who I am?"

"Yes, you are Henry Mitchell. You are here to breed with my wife."

"No, I am a prisoner like you and I intend to stop your wife... kill her if need be."

He reflected on this as I patiently waited to know his state of mind on the subject, fully prepared to strike him down if he said the wrong words. Finally, he shared his thoughts. "That's a good idea. I've been meaning to do that myself, just never got around to it."

"Then come with me. Now's your chance." He made no move to help himself, nor did he seem overly excited by his opportunity for escape. Was he sick in the head? Gamay had said he was. One thing was clear – something was wrong with him. Could have been a permanent mental condition or drug-induced, but either way Mr. Huckabee was a man defeated and resigned to follow the instructions of whoever happened to be in control of him at any given time.

Taking a dagger from a pile of them on the floor, I cut the connection rope from his ankles while wondering why he had never done so himself. And outside at the altar, the words of Wilma Huckabee pronounced sentence.

"Our sister Gamay has been possessed. We must crush the evil spirit from her wretched body."

A joyous shout of praise reverberated from outside the church hut, as I scanned the interior for items I might need. It was twice the size of the other structures and was connected on its back wall to a normal-sized hut, as though the larger was built onto the smaller. In the smaller were kept the child-slaves, Wilma saving the more spacious living for herself. In the larger were kept the weapons of darts, daggers and mixtures. Here too were Wilma's hanging-neatly western-style clothes and my piled-in-a-corner pilot's garb. Various religious hymnals, crosses and other implements of symbolism were stacked against a wall with one large Bible on top, and of particular interest were several wall-hanging pictures. One was of a church with a printed caption that read *United Church of Christ, Tupelo, Mississippi, 1933.* Another showed Simon and Wilma Huckabee standing on the front steps of that church in their Sunday-best attire, along with a handwritten farewell: *Best wishes to Brother and Sister Huckabee. May God be with you, as you spread the word of Jesus amongst the heathens. Dr. William Bishop.*

Lined along the floor, at least a dozen baskets were filled with her precious black pearls, and hanging above them, the ridiculous crown she wore when the pearls and not Jesus were at the forefront of her thoughts. Outside, the shriek of Gamay's voice rattled my bones and I silently crept close to the doorway, peeking past the edge in surveying the scene. While some still held my queen by her arms and legs, others had climbed onto the altar. They danced, walked and stomped upon Gamay's helpless body. Numbers were added, more joined in until I counted eight barefooted pygmies crushing my beautiful female. She grunted and moaned. She gasped for air, as more of her tribesmen stepped up to carry out Huckabee's sentence, and all the while, Boban, her chosen mate, stood silently outside the clamor, watching with eyes sad but doing nothing to help her.

Quickly, I bent down to gather my clothes, feeling inside my flight suit pocket to retrieve what I hoped was still there – Hank's fire, in the guise of a Zippo lighter. Eureka! I clutched it in my hand and flipped the lid, but before I could fire it up a sharp jab into the meat of my right butt cheek caused me to turn around, where Simon stood holding a blood-tipped dart between his bony fingers.

"I'm sorry, Mr. Mitchell, I've changed my mind." He frowned, shook his head and looked away as though ashamed. "The pygmy woman's oral service was pleasant, but I suppose I still love my wife, sad to say."

Simon nearly received a dagger to his belly before I collapsed to my knees, but he was such a pathetic creature that I could not bring myself to do it, and besides, there was no need to give that huckster spouse of his any more ammunition to use against me. The tranquilizer quickly took effect and Mr. Huckabee summoned the missus, his voice sounding distant and far removed, as though echoing from a cavernous auditorium. "Wilma, dear, that nice Navy man has come to pay us a visit."

From my knees I tilted to the left and landed softly on the matted floor, and then gently rolled to sprawl on my back. I was immobilized, but still conscious enough to recognize first the white-robed Wilma and then Boban, followed by the rest of the tribe. All who could fit entered the church hut. Words were spoken, but to me they were garbled, muffled, indecipherable. Activities of little humans buzzed all around me, but my only clear memory is the sight of Boban kneeling beside my chest and holding my hand in a gentle manner as though to comfort me. Juxtaposing this, Boban glared down at me with a ferocity that could kill, and with my last breath before losing consciousness altogether I mumbled to him.

"I did it for Gamay... and for you... Bobaaaaan..."

Huckabee's new angle was that I corrupted the innocent Gamay; that I taught her to remove Jesus's cross of protection and expose herself to evil; that I lured her into performing these acts of sin. What could I say? Guilty as charged and proud of it.

Even though it was my fault and not hers, Gamay still was to be further punished by banishment from the tribe. That it wasn't something more dramatic, I suspect, is because during the commotion over my capture the zealots left their victim unattended at the altar and she, my clever Gamay, had smartly made her escape into the forest. At least that part of my uprising was a success.

This was all explained to me by Wilma herself. I was forced to listen because now I was the victim laid upon her altar, fully conscious, fully naked and completely defenseless. This slab of stone was rectangular in shape and must have weighed tons. Probably beginning as a massive boulder from which the village was built around, the surface was sanded and smoothed to create this table two and one half feet in height. With a length of approximately six feet and width of three, the corners were blunted and sides angled slightly outward until the rock's base disappeared into the ground.

The Balingiga had awakened me with some sort of pungent herb stuffed into my nostrils, which immediately usurped the effects of tranquilizer kindly administered to me by the back stabber, Simon. Jolted to consciousness, I quickly realized that once again my wrists and ankles were wrapped in the now-familiar vine-woven rope. Stretched lengthwise on the altar and face-up, my heels rested on the surface near one end, while my hands were pulled beyond my head and positioned past the edge of the opposite end. The edge of stone slab made contact midway on my forearms. From there, the rest of my forearms to my wrists and hands dangled in air past the altar's edge. In between the bindings on my wrists and my ankles was a single rope connecting each to one another similar to the connector I'd seen on Simon's ankles, but mine were longer, each connecting rope about four feet long. The connector for the ropes binding my wrists was held in the palms of Boban, who stood on the ground past my head-end of the altar. He pulled on his rope to keep it taut, stretching my arms and forcing my forearms to lay flat upon the stone surface. Raising my head, I peered over my chest to the foot end where another Balingiga male stood holding the connector between my ankle bindings. He also pulled away from his end of the altar.

In essence, the good Christian woman Huckabee had transformed her sacred altar into a stretch rack with me as her victim. Glowing with piety in her white robe, she leaned forward and placed her hands into the middle of my stretched belly.

"Oh, heavenly father, why have you sent this evil man into our midst? What must we do to purify him of his sinful ways? Show me, o lord, so that I..."

"Shut the hell up," I spewed from the depths of my gut. "If you're going to torture me, torture me. If you're going to kill me, then do it, but I'm not going to listen to your ridiculous bullshit any longer."

The Balingiga gasped in horror, but not Wilma. She was unfazed by my outburst. First, she addressed the congregation. "Do not fear him, my children. The power of Jesus will protect us. He will help us chase the devil from this poor man's soul."

Then, she hovered over my face to address me with that soft, southern charm in a low volume only I could hear. "Well, well, Henry Mitchell, you certainly are a handful. I do believe you have caused enough trouble for one day. Perhaps after you've lost the use of your arms and legs, you won't think quite so highly of yourself."

She put both hands onto my chest and rubbed in small circles, all the while gazing up towards the sky. Plotting against me, while getting her jollies by touching my naked form, this vile woman was cold-hearted through and through. When her plans were finalized, she looked down, took each nipple between forefinger and thumb, then viciously twisted them, while telling of my fate.

"I thought a little stretching on the rack would satisfy my needs, but somehow it doesn't seem harsh enough. You are just too strong for your own good, Henry, dear." After releasing my nipples and transferring her left hand to my belly, she dug her fingertips deep into my muscle and emphasized her point. "Mmm, god damn, you are one tough son of a bitch."

Suddenly, she took away her hand and moved to the foot end of the altar, whispering something to the man holding my ankle connector. As for me, I caught Boban off guard with a violent yank of his connector rope. He stumbled towards me within my grasp, and as he did I clutched both of my hands onto his rib cage, lifted him into air and brought his inverted face directly above mine.

"I love you, Boban... mighty warrior."

A cluster of Balingiga men came to his rescue. They snatched him from my grip and returned him to earth. After quickly wrapping the connector rope around his hands, Boban moved backwards, pulling with all his strength to stretch me tighter than before.

With this move came a warning. "Do not be foolish, Mitchell. I would have killed you already, but the white woman wants you to live. Be happy torture is all you will get."

Spoken with authority, that's what I wanted to hear. Plus, Boban's calling Huckabee "the white woman" gave me hope for my future. After all, with Gamay wandering somewhere outside the village, Boban was about the only hope I had left.

While Boban and I were having our little interaction, other Balingiga were busy playing servants to Mrs. Huckabee. Between the small of my back and the top surface of altar they inserted a wooden log two feet in length and about three inches in diameter. It had been cut from a tree branch, and from overhanging limbs of a tree above me came a rustling produced by one male tribesmen, who dropped from the tree singular ends of two vine-ropes. A majestic tree it was, made to appear even more impressive by my laying-horizontal and looking-up view. Its massive trunk covered most of the ground between the church hut and its nearest regular-sized hut, while its height rose at least 60 feet into the air, but the man dropping ropes was perched upon a branch 30 feet up and directly above the altar. To this branch he tied his ends of the ropes.

Once the other ends reached the altar four men climbed onto its surface, two each standing on either side of my hips. Leaping, they grabbed hold their individual ropes two men per rope and swung like monkeys, bending down the branch while men standing on the ground tied each rope end to either end of the wooden log beneath me. They left no slack in the sections of rope between the bent branch above and log nestled in the small of my back. And the monkeys continued to hang.

Mrs. Huckabee took her position to my left between the altar and church, while the four hanging monkeys looked to her. She smiled, and then nodded her head. They released their ropes, dropping to the ground as the tree branch sprang up, returning to its desired position. And going with it was the log beneath the small of my back. Ungodly pain racked my body, as my middle-section violently thrust upwards, my arms and legs pulled in opposite directions and down. Boban held on tightly to the connecting rope between my wrists while the other man did the same at my ankles. My body formed a perfect curve, an upside-down U completely removed from the altar's stone surface. My heels and my fingers hovered inches above it, my wrists clasped to each other, my ankles clasped to each other. Wilma Huckabee had me in a three-way stretch – arms one way, legs the other, belly to the heavens.

No groans or grunts for this torture – I howled in agony. The instant shock of backward-curved spine and tightly stretched skin, muscles, joints and tendons racked me with pain and I literally screamed with each exhale of breath. But I am proud to say that after three or four of these falsetto cries, once the initial jolt was realized and fully felt, I was able to gather myself, strain my muscles to work against the ropes and lessen stress to my joints and tendons. Make no mistake, the pain was horrific and remained so, but my fighting back brought a bit of stabilization and my effort produced man sounds instead of woman sounds.

Seeing and hearing that I now was dealing with my torture, Wilma thought it a good time to taunt me. "There, that's much better. Can't have you screaming like a little girl. Can we? He-man? I think I'll call this my back-breaker stretch rack. Does it feel good?"

It was bad... real bad. My teeth clenched and I strained with all my might, pulling against Boban and the other man to keep my joints from tearing apart. Shards of sweat coated my skin, as I did battle with the tree branch. That damn thing was doing everything in its power to right itself, which caused my spine to nearly snap, feeling as though it were bent at an angle of 90 degrees if such a thing is possible. My diaphragm was stretched and flattened to its capacity. I struggled for air. The pressure on my compressed belly made it nearly impossible to breathe. It took every ounce of my strength just to gasp for small increments of oxygen, and I struggled to speak between stuttered inhales and exhales.

"What... do you... want from me?"

"Why, you silly man." She stood by one corner at my head-end of the altar so she could not only see my tormented face but also speak to me privately in her soft, sickeningly sweet voice. "Don't you know what I want?"

"I... I should've...killed you first... I could've... you know."

"Yes, well, that was a bad decision, wasn't it? Trying to save my silly husband."

I was coming apart, panting like an overheated canine. It was the only way I could breathe. An unforgiving tree branch fought me. A vile vixen tormented me. Two Balingiga men stretched me. Someone had driven spikes through every joint in my body. That was my pain, deep and nearly unbearable. Where was Gamay? With her nerve-numbing drug? No matter. Fighting my horrific agony was the only thing keeping my body together. I had to stay focused. I had to survive for as long as I possibly could. I had to hope that one Balingiga would think for himself, come to his senses and take back what was rightly his.

"Boban... Balingiga chieftain... make her... stop."

"You cause this, Mitchell." Boban could see my face and I his. He was unmoved by my words, unconcerned with my desperate struggle to survive – my tightly clenched face and teeth; my sweat running in streams down the length of my chest and arms, dripping off of my scalp and fists in buckets; my horrifically stretched chest and belly, muscles flexed and laterals flared wide with expansion. Neither sad nor angry, Boban sat on the ground straining against me with my stretching rope firmly in his grip. "I will do nothing for you."

"What did you call him?" Huckabee jumped in. "Balingiga? Who told you that word? Gamay? That little traitor."

My only victory so far. My beautiful Gamay.

"She... remembers. She... knows... ... You are... false."

"Sure she does, thanks to you. I should have kept you gagged. What was I thinking? Oh, well, it doesn't matter. Boban is smart. He knows Jesus is on my side."

Ignoring her, I focused on Boban. He did not like her words. The strain on his face went beyond his effort to keep me stretched. Boban scowled at her. Her back was turned to him so she did not see it, but I did, and with a renewed energy I defied her torture.

"Jesus... loves... all people... Gamay... me... Boban... even you... that's... what I believe... So... why are you... doing this... to me?"

Agitated, she stormed to the center of the altar and stepped up to clutch my penis in her hand. "For this, you stupid man." She let go of me, jumped down and returned to the corner of stone where only she and I could hear her words, spoken with an evil whisper.

"You saw my husband. Do you think I'd want my children to come from that? No. You were a godsend. A real man. A strong, virile, white man falls out of the sky and I told myself right then and there that I would have your seed. But I knew you'd be trouble. I knew you'd fight me and I was right. So, that's why I'm doing this. When I'm finished with you, that glorious cock will be the only part of you that still works. I'm going to make it so you'll never walk again, never use your arms again. Hell, I might even cut out your tongue so you'll never talk again. I'm going to rip you to pieces, Henry Mitchell. I'll have your chest, belly, dick, balls and semen. That's all I want. I won't be needing the rest."

Between my agony and her insanity, I groaned, grunted and howled with rage. "That's it? ... You... want to fuck? ... You... torture me... so... you can... fuck me? Cut me loose... I'll... fuck... fuck your brains out... lady... Let's go."

"No, sir, it's too late. You can't keep your big mouth shut. You must be broken first. And I will break you, Captain Henry Mitchell. I'll store you away just like Simon, a disposable slab of meat. The pygmies will forget all about you. I'll fuck you when I get the notion and raise our... *my* children the rest of the time. Then, when they're old enough, we'll take our pearls and leave you two with these savages to fend for yourselves. What a glorious day it will be when I can get away from this god-forsaken hell hole."

She left me and climbed onto the altar. "In fact, let's get started right now."

At her summons, the Balingiga tribe surrounded and stood on the altar to assault my tortured body. She had them all, men and women, put their mouths to any piece of my skin they could find, saving my penis for herself.

Wilma Huckabee sucked on me, while countless lips and tongues licked away my sweat. A married Christian woman was sucking my dick. Surely to god it wasn't going to work. How could a man possibly perform under such conditions? I suffered in unholy agony, my pain nearly causing me to long for death, or at least unconsciousness. Arousal, sexual stimulation was the furthest thing on my mind. I loathed this woman. Surely she knew it, but still, Wilma Huckabee sucked on me while torturing me.

It is beyond the use of words to describe what it's like to have your dick sucked while being stretched on the rack. The opposition of sensations, unyielding pain versus ecstatic pleasure, cannot be understood unless experienced, but I do not recommend it. Add to this the humiliation felt when your body is mercilessly tortured and lovingly worshiped at the same time, all against your will, and it is all a man can do to cling to his sanity. A man's penis responds whether he wants it to or not. Mine did. With lips kissing every part of me, tongues licking the brine from me as quickly as I could produce it, and a female mouth slavishly worshiping my phallus, my erection came despite my wishes.

Wilma spit out and manually clutched my hardened tool. She instructed a tribesman to lay on the altar at her feet, using him to elevate herself. She inserted me to her vaginal opening underneath her robe, and then took me inside.

I was crushed and I shuddered. Ecstasy tried to dominate me, but pain would not surrender. I was her tool, unable to withdraw, unable to enjoy. This was Wilma's show and I was resigned to suffer on my torture rack until she'd taken what she wanted.

With Balingiga worshiping her victim, Wilma motivated herself by scrutinizing my racked body and verbally expressing her approval.

"Oh, yeah... flex those big muscles, you beautiful man. Oh, god, you are gorgeous." She angled my cock head to target her clit, and then impaled herself upon me, ramming my tool to the depths of her pussy. "Oh, god damn... I've never seen a man take punishment like you can. Let me hear you grunt. Let me hear your pain, you god damned animal."

She frantically screwed herself with my tool, bumping her clittie against my bulging mushroom again and again rapid-fire, but still she was not satisfied. Stripping off her robe, she flung it past the end of the alter, where it fell to the ground near the feet of Boban.

"Stretch him more," the naked woman shouted from her altar pole. "You two, pull with all your strength. Make my man suffer for this pussy. Make him scream like a bitch."

Boban and his counterpart leaned back to end me. I was in hell, worse than hell, but come hell or high water I would not scream for her. I would die first, a very real possibility.

Wilma Huckabbe meant nothing now. I couldn't feel her, her pussy, or her tongue-licking servants. All was pain. All was near-suffocation. All was near unconsciousness. My vision blurred and a bright light turned all I could see to white. Death was near. This had to be my tunnel, the one of which I'd read, the one of which those who'd nearly passed and come back had described in nearly identical details – but no, this was no tunnel. A squinting of my eyes enabled me to find the source of light. On the ground next to Boban, my Zippo, a streak of sunlight reflecting directly from its silver-plated cover to my pupils. He'd held my hand for purpose, taken it from me in the church hut. He'd hidden it in his loin cloth, but with his final thrust to stretch me to death my precious Zippo had presented itself.

"Boban!" I gasped to speak. "You... make... fire."

"What?"

"Look... beside you."

As Huckabee continued riding my pole, oblivious to our conversation, Boban looked to his left, then to his right, where he spotted the silver box. "I took it from you. It is mine."

"Yes... it... makes... fire... Boban... makes... fire."

He let go the rope with his right hand and held on with his left, which allowed the branch to lift me up just a bit, then Boban picked up the lighter and with a mighty gulp of air I gave him instructions in singular phrases.

"Open it with your thumb." I mimicked the motion with my thumb and he flipped open the lid. "Turn the wheel fast." Again I showed him the motion and he sparked the flame.

Boban, startled, released his rope and suddenly one-third of the stretch rack was broken. The tree branch sprang up to where it wanted to go bringing both the log and top half of my body with it. Like a catapult, the apparatus immediately sprang my body to vertical. I stood near the foot-end of the altar while my Balingiga worshipers flew from the slab in all directions. The slingshot continued towards the sky, tree branch taking it over my head and arms as though stripping off a t-shirt. Wilma also went flying. My violent ascension disconnected her from my cock and sent her through the air off the foot-end of the altar, where she crashed atop the tribesman still holding my ankle connector rope.

Within seconds, I was taken from the torturous state of being ripped apart to a dominating position standing above the tribe. Immediately, I wheeled to point at the Zippo.

"Look, your Balingiga chief makes fire!"

Boban stood with lighter in hand, a glorious flame illuminating his stunned expression. Each and every one of the Balingiga fell to their knees, hailing the rebirth of their tribal leader. "Boban! Boban! Boban!"

Huckabee struggled to her feet. Naked and nervous, she desperately tried to regain control. "No, my children, it is false. It is a fire of the devil." She pointed to me. "He brought it here to trick you."

"No, white woman. You are false." Boban, the warrior, reached down to pick up her discarded robe. He brought its cloth to his flame. "The fire of Boban is true. Watch."

A hushed awe enveloped the village, as the white garment with red cross quickly became a foul-smelling, smoke billowing inferno. Fully confident in his abilities, Boban tossed the burning cloth aside and stepped to his left, putting the Zippo's flame onto dried leaves of the church hut. "This god is not Balingiga. Boban brings fire to the white woman's false god."

Like a tender box, the parched, dead foliage and wood inhaled Boban's flame. It rapidly spread along the side wall and continued to the roof, at which time Wilma Huckabee, panicked that she might lose the only thing that mattered to her, streaked into the burning structure. Returning quickly with two baskets of black pearls clutched in her arms, she ran back for more but was blocked at the entrance by her pitiful husband.

Simon Huckabee's hair was afire. The pitiful man frantically tried to extinguish it by smashing his head with the palms of his hands. Worsening his plight, his thoughtful wife had ordered that his ankles again be bound with rope after my capture so that now he could only shuffle with baby steps in his attempt to escape the inferno.

Mrs. Huckabee had no concern for him or his problems. Tragically, she pushed the stricken man back to clear the path to her precious pearls. "Out of my way, you idiot." With screams of horror and agony, he tumbled back into raging fire.

Neither Simon nor Wilma Huckabee were seen again. Neither I nor the Balingiga made any attempts to save them. Instead, we watched in wonder as the roof collapsed, taking the cross of a false Jesus with it. And as a final gesture to rid his people of what was, Boban picked up the two baskets filled with precious, black pearls and tossed them into the infernal pile, burying them along with the greed, cruelty and lies from which they came.

Restoration

My love queen of the pygmies called out from the direction of the stream, but it was not Mitchell's name that was heard. It was the name of Boban. Into the village clearing came the children of the Balingiga, followed closely by the beautiful Gamay, who had during her banishment and my torture summoned each pearl diver out of the cave. Gamay brought them home to stay.

As the children rejoined their rightful caretakers in celebrated reunion, Boban, Gamay and I celebrated by seeking out all Jesus-related relics that remained in the village. When we found one, we threw it onto the still-smouldering ruins of the church hut. All Balingiga men, women and children stripped away their loin cloths and added them to the flames, freeing themselves forever from the shackles of shame introduced by western hypocrites.

Boban gathered his men to organize a hunt, while Gamay and three women of her choosing took me to the home of their chief for recuperation. The lingering pain of my stretch rack continued to punish the sockets of my arms and legs, until the women laid me down on my belly to massage my joints, muscles and tendons with a deep, penetrating salve concocted by Gamay. No English words were spoken, unless addressed to me, and the females nearly had me put to sleep when Boban burst into the hut, shouting in his language and frantically waving his arms. After he and Gamay exited, it was told to me that all poisons and darts had been destroyed in the fire, and so like the legacy of the Balingiga themselves, everything started anew.

Gamay and the other women gathered what was needed to make poison, while Boban and his men made new darts using feathers that through the years had been saved as trophies and hung on the walls of their living huts.

That evening, after a long and peaceful afternoon nap for me and my three nurses, the tribe celebrated, feasting on roasted birds and their favorite of all rainforest prizes, monkey meat. As for myself, I preferred pig, but gladly pretended to enjoy their delicacy.

The next several days were busy ones, as I helped them put their lives back together. First, we crossed the stream and gathered at the entrance of the cave to close its opening, filling its mouth with boulders as big as we could carry until it no longer resembled the entrance of a cave.

Next, we began to clear away debris from the ruins of the church hut. Whatever bits and pieces of its contents had survived the fire were thrown onto the open flame in the village clearing, regardless of whether it had been a possession of the white woman or the tribe. As for my belongings, only one item was of importance, and that was my metal Navy identification tag. Coated with sealant to survive almost anything, we did find it intact and I clutched the precious dog tag in my hand, thankful to have proof that I still was indeed Captain Henry Mitchell.

The site of these ruins would be the foundation of a new home – that of the Balingiga chief Boban, his queen Gamay and their children, the first seed of which most likely was planted that first night of celebration when they were free to love one another with no white woman rules. Or I suppose it could have been done the night of my captivity when Gamay screwed Boban with me staked out nearby and watching. Or I suppose it's best that I not think of the other possibility.

The festivities of restoration were a grand affair. Conducted around the village fire near the slab of stone with smoldering church ruins as a backdrop, there was monkey meat a-plenty, succulently roasted fowl, raw berries and nuts, plus a beverage made from berries with a powerful taste not far removed from very strong coffee. In fact, if I didn't know better I'd swear this drink gave me a caffeine rush. More likely though, it was a rush of pure happiness, the sense of victory and accomplishment we all felt.

Children were allowed to play and be children. Men chose their desired mates and reunited, soon to make up for time lost. And Boban was officially made chief by the tribal elder, who presented a necklace long hidden away, a stringing together of twelve intricately carved wooden heads, representations of ancient Balingiga. With Boban standing surrounded by his kneeling tribe, the elder raised the necklace for all to see, and then lowered it past Boban's head and onto his shoulders.

This concluded the evening's public festivities, but the making up for time lost part I mentioned earlier continued until daybreak, some in huts, others right there in the open clearing near the village fire.

I belonged to Boban and Gamay. They kept me in their hut, and although there were no public accolades for my good deeds in helping them to free themselves and their people from Huckabee, my private rewards quickly made me forget whatever hurt feelings I might have had.

Gamay insisted I lay on my back. She never told me this. She told Boban in their language, and I was pleased that they abandoned mine. Nothing was required to coerce my erection. As soon as Gamay touched me I sprang to life, for I'd longed to feel her touch since she'd left me staked spread eagle so many hours ago. She straddled me, inserted me while sitting on my thighs with her upper torso vertical. Standing before her was Boban, his feet on either side of my rib cage, his butt towards me, his cock dangling before his love queen's lips. She did it all. Her men did nothing. Gamay targeted herself with my penis, gliding up my pole and back down while slavishly worshiping her man with her lips and tongue. We were free to express our joy – they in their Balingiga tongue, English for me, but for the most part our language was universal. We spoke with moans of pleasure, groans of exertion, grunts of lust and cries of orgasm. The language of sex; the expressions of mutual admiration;

all were spoken freely and at volumes of our own choosing, our own desires.

It is possible that Gamay slipped one of her famous aphrodisiacs into our food or drink, but I doubt it. Years of want dictated the happenings in our hut. Without interruption, Gamay and Boban reconfigured themselves upon me so that I could receive her oral praise while he basked in the warmth of her loving vagina. Boban sat on my chest facing my feet. Leaning backwards, he draped himself atop my head, the small of his back resting upon my turned cheek, and from this position Gamay mounted him. With Boban's legs spread wide and his heels on the matted floor, Gamay inserted his penis while on her hands and knees, and then she lowered her breasts onto my belly, taking my cock into her mouth to service me.

Our Balingiga queen was so very skilled, as she used her lifting and lowering knees to hump her man, used her twisting and turning neck to suck her guest. So grateful was I that they'd accepted me, included me in the love they shared; so ecstatic was I that they'd instantly cast aside the suppression they had endured as though forgotten, something with which I in no small way played a role; that without thinking I clasped my hands onto Boban's stretched-atop-me belly and rubbed him there. Was man touching man forbidden? Certainly under the old rule, but not now. Boban tightened his muscles and I deep-massaged him, his woman's inner thighs slamming the tops of my hands. I slid my palms up his stomach and onto his chest. With rapid rubbing, I heated his chest, stomach and belly with frantic friction, and with an ear-piercing howl Boban fired his load into his woman.

He stayed there, gasping, as Gamay finished me. We both remained stacked until Gamay finished herself, and then we three untangled. With Boban on my right, his head nestled in the crook of my arm pit, and Gamay on my left, her head resting on my chest, we basked in our afterglow. I wrapped my arms around both of them, rubbed their shoulders with my hands, and this is how we slept.

Or at least I did. They woke me up numerous times, because off to the side and by themselves Boban and Gamay fucked all night long. My dreams were pure pleasure, inspired by the ecstatic moans, grunts and howls of two lovers. They, like all other members of the Balingiga tribe were making up for time lost.

The next day brought rain to the rainforest. I learned that when water falls the tribe does nothing. It is a time to stay home where they eat stored plants, nuts and berries, formerly their staple diet along with raw monkey meat, all before the gift of fire. Their only duty is for the fire. The village flame is covered with a high-arcing lean-to made of the same materials as those of the huts, which reminded me that Boban and I should have a conversation about this powerful necessity.

Huddled together in the dry warmth of his home, I asked him about this. "Boban, where is the fire?" I made the flicking motion with my thumb.

"Here, Mitchell," he retrieved it from a hiding place under the floor matting. "It is yours. You take it."

"No, Boban, it is yours. You saved me... saved all of us with this lighter. You must keep it, but I must show you something."

With Gamay sitting silently and obediently by his side, Boban handed my Zippo to me, but before flipping open its lid I gave it a quick inspection, perhaps a visual goodbye kiss. Zippos are handsome and handy little items, and this one – with its smooth and shiny silver-colored plating, U.S. Navy insignia monogrammed to one side, H. Mitchell scripted to the other – had been my trustworthy friend since its purchase from my boot camp PX back in Illinois. Gifting it to Boban meant more to me than it did to him, but nonetheless I flipped it open, removed the inside cartridge from its cover, turned it over and put my finger onto the felt padding.

"Here, Boban, touch this."

He poked it with his index finger. "It is wet."

"Yes, the wet makes flame stay." Next, I flipped it over and turned the wheel. "This makes spark to start fire... wet keeps fire lit."

He watched my demonstration. "Yes, I remember."

"Boban, this wet will go dry... four days... maybe five... no more fire. I don't have any more wet. No more wet... lighter will not work."

Disappointed, he lowered his head. "No fire, Boban is not chief."

"Did the white woman show you how to make fire?"

"She started with little sticks. She scraped against box they came in and made fire. One day, she tells us fire must always burn, because it is the fire of Jesus."

I chuckled to myself. Wilma worried that she was running out of matches. "Boban, when rain stops, I will show you how to make fire from rock."

That didn't happen until three days later, but it was time well-spent. The men braved the deluge collecting wood. In their huts they restocked their supply of weapons by making more darts, having only initially made enough for their celebration-day hunt. The women did the same in restocking plants and whatever else was needed to make mixes.

After announcing to the tribe that he was taking Mitchell to learn the hunt, Boban and I left the village in search of the flint rock he would need. He patiently waited for me to negotiate undergrowth and rocks with my civilized, tender bare feet until we found a good-sized deposit. After building a small mound of brush, leaves and wood I demonstrated for Boban the clicking together of flint rocks to ignite a flame and make a campfire. Next we filled our baskets with flint rocks to take home, and then Boban brought down a few birds from the trees to make our lie a truth before our return to the village.

I showed them how and helped them build a structure of wood and stacked stones to cover the village fire, complete with chimney to channel smoke up instead of everywhere. This became their eternal flame, dedicated to one of their gods whose name I don't remember and is not important. The god was Balingiga, that is all that mattered. Represented by a statue carved of wood, it was resurrected from its hiding place in the home of the tribe elder. Why Wilma Huckabee allowed them to keep the statue and necklace I did not know, so I asked him.

"I know she is bad," he explained in weak voice. "Because she take eyes." Undoubtedly, the two empty curvatures made for sockets once held two black pearls, plucked by a greedy white witch. "I keep for us," he continued. "I pray to him. Tell him to make bad woman go away."

And their god did make her go away, although it took him twelve years to get around to it.

Neither I nor the Balingiga ever again brought up the subject of Wilma and Simon Huckabee. I never investigated the purpose of their missionary assignment, why they came to this island, nor how they found the Balingiga and survived without being made into monkey meat. I suspect that box of matches is what saved them, and I also suspect their intentions were initially good even though I don't agree with forcing one's beliefs on others. In my readings of the words attributed to Jesus from an historical, unemotional perspective, his philosophy says to live it, not talk it. Those who are ready will get it and follow your example of their own volition. Those who aren't won't notice you.

My guess is that plucking those eyes from their statue changed everything. Once Wilma learned the location of their source, all good intentions were cast into what she called the fire of Jesus. To hell with the pygmies and Jesus and my husband, thought she. I'm going to be a millionairess.

During the construction of our new eternal flame we paused for a few seconds, interrupted by a strange changing of the air all around us, almost as though the humidity had been sucked out of it. Not knowing the cause of this, we resumed our work and thought nothing more of it.

Little did I know that this signaled the end of one global conflict and beginning of another. What I did know was that the pygmies were well on their way to once again living as the mighty Balingiga and that it was time for me to resume doing what I was trained to do – time for me to rejoin my Navy pilots and the battle from which I'd been taken.

They outfitted me for the journey with a newly-made loin cloth and sandals, soles made of boar hide and connections of sturdy, vine-woven ropes, the same as those used to once keep me in bondage. With one monkey-hide pouch filled of food stuffs and another filled with flint rocks strapped over one shoulder, a dagger in one hand and my Navy dog tag in the other, I left the peaceful village of my Balingiga friends. There were no heartfelt goodbyes or hugs and kisses. To them, that should only lead to sex, and while I was tempted to stay there forever to mostly do just that, I did not trust myself. I, like Wilma Huckabee, knew the value of those pearls and in time, I, like Wilma Huckabee, might also entertain foolish ideas of taking what was theirs for my own gain.

And so, they merely pointed me in the direction from which the Huckabees had come and I was on my way.

For six days I had been absent from the civilized world, and I had no clue as to whether Japanese soldiers were on the island or not, but remembering the sky view from the cockpit of my failing Grumman, I estimated a four-day journey to reach the ocean.

Three days later, with no incidents of importance to retell (except for another one of those strange alterations of air around me, my experience of the destruction of Nagasaki) I arrived at the coast facing unseen Luzon. Although a risk, I started a fire to attract rescue from either friend or foe not knowing that a ceremony was soon to take place on the USS Missouri officially ending the War in the Pacific. Two days later, a U.S. Navy weather aircraft saw my smoke. I stripped, gathered everything the

Balingiga had given to me and buried it. When a Navy cruiser broke the horizon next day that's how they found me, sitting on narrow beach next to my fire with my dog tag necklace as my only attire.

During my debriefing, the commanding investigator seemed a bit skeptical that I'd managed to fend for myself twelve days with no weapons and no protection. That I'd survived on berries and small amphibians was plausible enough; that my flight suit shredded and was left in the tree seemed to wash; even the story of my shoe removal in order to climb down from my tree passed muster. No, the problem he had is that I was a bit too healthy-looking, not quite as gaunt as I should be, and had he taken a fecal sample he would have known that I'd dined quite well lately, thank you. But he didn't do that, nor did he order a fact-finding flight patrol to where I'd been. That would need to be a high priority mission, which this was not. Everybody wanted to go home and most of us were.

And so did I.

PART TWO –
Doing My Duty
What's Expected of a Man

Now, you will notice that the details of my saga are becoming scarce, and I'm sure you'll understand that just because I mentioned Luzon and the Philippines doesn't mean they're anything other than a reference point. My island's in the South Pacific. That's good enough. My tribe is the Balingiga if memory serves me correctly, but maybe it doesn't. I believe those pearls are black, if indeed they are pearls. After all, I'm old, weary and sometimes forgetful.

The Navy duly noted longitude and latitude of this speck of land from which I was plucked, and in 1956 the government of the nearest country to the island claimed it for themselves with no protests from the rest of the world. They set up a research station on its coast, mostly for radio relays of weather concerns or distress signals from ships or airplanes – a one man operation. Fortunately, the location was opposite the coast from where I'd been rescued and by my estimation far-removed from where I guessed my village to be. Nothing more was done and further news of the island disappeared, but still I monitored this daily.

My after-war life in the U.S. was pleasant enough. I finished the high school courses necessary to get my GED. I married a girl remembered from high school days, settled in Chicago and retired from the floor of the Mercantile Exchange. Our bedroom life never strayed from the norm. Our two kids grew up like most WASP baby-boomers – healthy, mostly-happy and provided for financially, culturally and psychologically.

My family attended church, the wife insisted on it, but at the same time I insisted we only go to the Sunday night services in a congregation whose minister was laid back and positive.

In other words, I did everything I was supposed to do until the kids were grown and on their own and both of my parents were dead. Then, I divorced their mother – 1982; I retired from the Merc. – 1987; and got me a home computer to trade futures contracts for myself.

Please don't think I didn't enjoy myself during these years. Chicago's the greatest sports town in the world and nothing thrilled me more than taking my son to see the Blackhawks and Bears do their amazing things, not to mention sharing with both my children whatever I know enough about to be worth telling them.

My daughter's like her mother – meddlesome, but in a good way. She actively participates for causes in which she believes. She proudly was taken away in paddy wagon during the 1968 Democratic Convention in our town. And get this, she married an airline pilot who flies out of O'Hare, an occupation for which I was easily qualified but declined to follow. Jet engines were already on the horizon, which would require a whole new training process for Hank. I knew commodities, grew up on a farm. It was a perfect fit and I never regretted staying grounded.

I figured Uncle John to be disappointed in me for this, but he wasn't. He continued his crop dusting business happy to know that I was happy in what I was doing. He refused to upgrade from his Jenny, even though parts became more and more difficult to find. What he couldn't order and what I couldn't find for him through my Navy connections he built himself, but that engine all went at once, literally shook loose into a hundred pieces while Uncle John was at 800 feet. I'm proud that my children met him, learned from him and remember him. They understand and appreciate the important role he played in shaping their father, who in turn shaped them.

Whereas I wanted off the farm, my son loved it. Many of his weekends and all of his youthful summers were spent there hunting with my father, learning how to garden from my mother. He eagerly listened to Errol Mitchell's every word on how to rotate crop fields, breed and raise beef cattle, take them to market, repair tractors, combines, the house and outbuildings, plant, fertilize and harvest anything that could be grown legally to make money. Not only did he listen, he participated, and when both Errol and Helena Mitchell were gone from this earth, my son took over operation of my inheritance, and there he still resides with wife and four offspring.

No, you won't get any complaints from me regarding my life here, it's just that Boban, Gamay and their people were always in my thoughts every day, so with the completion of my domestic obligations I cleared the way for me to go back, if indeed the day ever came when I should.

Daily, I news-searched the world-wide web, MSNing and/or Googling the name given to the island, its coordinates, and even the words "black pearls" to see what might show up.

Nothing.

So it stumped me good when in 2005 I got a call from the Veteran's Administration telling me a Wilbur Carson was trying to make contact with me. Nervous, I took the phone number he'd left with them for me to call, dialing while trying to remember the name. Old shipmate? Former pilot? Unknown fund raising solicitor?

"Hello, I'm returning a call to Wilbur Carson. Name's Mitchell."

"Hank Mitchell? How ya' been, buddy?"

"Adequate. You?"

"Don't remember me... do ya'?"

"Afraid not."

"The USS Raleigh... 1945... we plucked you off that island... I debriefed you."

"Of course. Now, I remember. How's things?"

He told me his post-war life story, prying what he could out of me regarding mine. A widower with one grown son, Wilbur Carson made his career with the Portland, Oregon police department, retiring a detective. This I thought did not bode well for me, and when he finally got around to the purpose of his business I knew that he'd been way too busy.

"I have something in my possession that might interest you."

"What."

"It's a handwritten letter... hard to read, but dated 1936."

"And?"

"It's signed by a Simon Huckabee. Ring a bell?"

"Not really. What's it about?"

"It's a plea for help... about some island at longitude such and such and latitude... well, it just seems awfully close to that island you were on."

"So?"

"So, according to him, there's plenty of humans there... not to mention a few... shall we say... precious valuables."

"Sounds interesting. How do you know it's the same island?"

"Oh, come on now, Captain Mitchell." The detective's tone got a bit testy and I suppose the addressing me as Captain was to remind me of his 1945 skepticism. "There's no other piece of land anywhere close. Stop being coy and let me show you the letter. You'll see that playing stupid won't work with me."

"Ok, if that'll make you happy. Where do you want to hook up?"

Because it made me feel better, I forced him to come to Chicago. Gave him the name and address of a quiet diner I know, plus the date and time to show up.

Ain't that a pisser? I spend the better part of sixty years looking for any information about my island, and this palooka stumbles across an old letter for sale online written by Simon Huckabee himself. Seems that before his wife went completely nuts and tethered him to the church hut Simon recognized that his future looked rather bleak, and so he wrote down details of his plight, dropped it into an empty fifth of whiskey bottle that his wife liked to drink but nobody else knew about, jammed in the cork and slipped out of the village for five or six days to toss his bottle into the ocean.

After drifting around for a year or two the bottle washed ashore somewhere near Bangkok, Siam and was found by a woman in a fishing village. Not knowing English, she stuffed the letter back into its bottle, corked it and stored it away, never to be seen again until 1996 when the woman's grandson found it going through her belongings upon her death. He turned it over to the U.S. Embassy in Bangkok, Thailand, where upon seeing mention made of Huckabee's church, embassy staff packed the bottle and contents for air shipment and sent it to the Tupelo, Mississippi United Methodist Church in Christ. Nobody at the church knew of the Huckabees or of any such mission to the Pacific. There were no records to confirm any of it, including previous employment of a Dr. William Bishop, and so the current minister, assuming it was some sort of hoax and not noticing the extra word on the address label not contained in Simon's letter, kept it for himself until he retired, and in his retirement he found that buying and selling at online auctions was an interesting and sometimes profitable hobby, so he put the bottle and letter up for sale just to see what would happen, making mention of the island coordinates written by Simon and, PRAISE THE LORD!, Wilbur Carson took it off his hands.

In a 1960's vintage booth at the Bluebird Diner on East Ohio Street in Chicago, Illinois, I strained to read the faded blue ink of Simon's sloppy hand. Knowing how Wilma and Simon Huckabee met their end made reading Simon's words from nine years prior a rather painful experience, but it was all there – her taking two pearls from the wooden statue, her discovery of the cave and abundance of pearls at the bottom of the cave's waters; her twisting of their original purpose to teach the heathens the words of Jesus Christ; and of the gradual descent into her mad obsession to possess each and every one of those pearls no matter how many pygmies died in the process. He gave the coordinates where he thought they were, and although inaccurate they were close enough. He did not tell of how they learned of the island, why they went there or how they got there, but he did say that he was dropping two pearls into the bottle to prove his need for rescue was genuine.

"So, Wilbur. Where are the two pearls?"

"Are you kidding? Probably in Thailand."

"Your seller didn't know?"

"Nope."

"Do you honestly believe any of this?"

"I don't know. You tell me."

"You're the investigator. Did you try to find out about Simon Huckabee from Tupelo, Mississippi? There must be some sort of birth records or something."

At this point he gathered the letter and carefully folded its original creases. "Whatever I know I'm keeping to myself until you tell me what you know. It's like this, Mitchell. For sixty years I've had a hunch about you. That's how I operate... hunches. You lied then and you're lying now. Don't think I didn't check it out before coming back to the States. Called in a whole bunch of favors to get me a pilot for a Duck ride over the island."

"And?"

"Didn't see a god damned thing... except for green. Even had the fella set down in the ocean near where we picked you up. Took me a swim to shore."

"And?"

He opened his briefcase and pulled out a plastic bag, dumping its contents onto the table. God, it smelled to high heaven, but was still intact – my monkey-hide pouch, the one in which I'd toted the flint rocks to start my distress-signal fire. I looked but did not touch, and then I looked at Carson but did not speak. With a sigh he reached again into his briefcase and brought out my dagger.

"There's more, Captain Mitchell. Should I continue?"

"Why don't you put 'em online? Auction 'em off?"

"Ok, look, pal. There's no friggin' way you made all this shit by yourself. It's like this. I'm going to find those pearls. Everything fits. Either you can help me, or I'll raise the money and take an expedition myself. Take me to the village. We'll split 50-50. Otherwise, it'll take every dime I have to buy the equipment and people I'll need, but so help me god I'll do it... and I will find them."

Poor guy. I guess a policeman's pension wasn't good enough. Our waitress stopped by to tell us in her classic north-side nasal-whine to "put away that crap on the table 'cause you're makin' the customers puke," which gave me time for some decision making.

I figured it was just a matter of time before one of those satellite feeds free to use online would include views of my island and that eventually somebody, somewhere would see my village and make themselves famous. Wilbur seemed hell-bent on going and by my way of thinking it'd be much easier to control the situation with him alone. Sure, he might spend his life-savings to fund an expedition without me that found nothing, but more than likely he would eventually find the village and his pearls. How would I ever know either way if I wasn't there with him? Keep your friends close and your enemies closer, so they say. I listened to his plan.

Just imagine it – two men in their middle eighties traveling secretly halfway around the world in search of treasure. We flew out of San Francisco for Manila; there rented an auto for a drive to Aparri; there purchased a fine-looking Ocean Master 31-footer boat, along with food, water and some carry-on fuel containers for an extra 100 gallons. I made him purchase a boat because he couldn't really afford it and I could, but he did put up a bit of protest.

"Hank, my plan was to charter."

"Well, gee, detective. Won't it be harder to track us if you buy one? Besides, what are you going to tell 'em when they ask how many days you want it and where you're taking it?"

It gave me great pleasure to observe his tortured expression as he counted out nearly all of his converted-to-peso cash, but hey, he's the one who chose the boat he wanted. We arrived on the side of the island where the Navy picked me up, its appearance unchanged 60 years later – except that my flint rocks had of course washed away.

"Should we beach her or drop anchor?" Wilbur wanted to know.

"Better find a cove and beach it. Cover her up best we can."

I watched every move he made and had done so since meeting him at the San Francisco terminal. We'd traveled light – all carry-ons, and our inspections of each other's bags were much more thorough than that of the airport security staff.

Wilbur Carson assured me that he had kept all information a secret, only he and I knew of our adventure and I believed him. He had that look in his eye, that same demeanor I'd seen in the person of Wilma Huckabee. Greed drove this 80-something year-old man to move like he was 40 and he intended to share his treasure with no one. When the time came that I was no longer of use to him that would be the end of me, if he could figure out a way to do me in.

We found a small inlet about half a nautical mile from my beach. We beached it, anchored it and covered it with foliage taken from the edge of rainforest.

"Shall we, Hank?"

"We shall, Wilbur."

Tits Don't Sag

Ahhh! That ungodly heat! Two men our age don't move very fast in air so thick you can hardly breathe it, but at least I dressed properly. My Carhartt khaki cargo shorts gave my legs freedom to step upgrade or downgrade with ease, Wilbur's denim jeans did not. And why on earth he wore a nylon-lined windbreaker jacket in this sauna was beyond me, unless he felt a need to protect his arms. At least he got the shoes and shirt parts right, but still I slowed my pace so that he could keep up with me. Needless to say, nothing much was recognizable to me but I did have a compass and a good sense of retracing my direction in the forest, based on what I remembered of my journey out, along with angles of the cathedral effect from sunlight through canopy. Without this I lacked confidence, and so we did not travel at night.

Compared to me Wilbur was a physical wreck, and the thought did cross my mind that in his vulnerable, huffing and puffing state I could easily strangle him, go back to sink the boat and live happily ever after. Fortunately for him, I am not of such mind-set. With such guilt upon me, there could be no happily ever after, and so we trudged onward through five sunsets when about mid-day on the sixth I knew Wilbur and I were not alone. Those clicking sounds were neither fowl nor beast. My Balingiga were here at ground level and above us, communicating with one another in the same manner as they did that night I sat on tree branch in flight suit.

"Wilbur," I whispered, my arm back and hand on his chest. "Don't move... don't make a sound. They're here."

We both stood silent, as I removed my Navy dog tag necklace. "Balingiga warriors!" I shouted. "I am friend of Boban... Balingiga chief... Boban... Gamay..."

The clicking stopped and I waited. Perhaps Boban was no more, but still his name would be known. And perhaps my name would be remembered. "Balingiga... I am Captain Henry Mitchell... friend of Boban... friend of Gamay... Boban... Balingiga chief... Gamay... woman of Boban... Captain Henry Mitchell... Gamay... Bo..."

"Boban no more." The voice came from above, behind me and to my right. Slowly I turned to find its source, knowing that at any second a blow dart lethal or otherwise could penetrate my neck. About 20 feet up and 10 feet away the face of a male warrior peered through tree foliage. I held up my dog tag and spoke.

"Gamay... no more?"

"You," he thrust his finger out of leaf and into the open, pointing at me. Mitchell?"

I pointed to my chest. "Mitchell... yes... friend of Boban... and Gamay."

The warrior jumped down from his tree, signaling to others with mouthed clicks. As he approached, I whispered to Wilbur for him not to move or speak, and when the warrior stood before me within a two foot distance and his face level with my belly, I again spoke.

"Gift... for Gamay." I pointed to my cargo shorts, right front flapped pocket. Cautiously, he reached in to take my gift – a Zippo purchased in 1945 at the Subic Bay PX with the same U.S. Navy insignia and scripted H. Mitchell as the one left behind for Boban's fire. He held it, inspected it, opened its lid, flipped the flint wheel and lit the flame. With eyes bright, he fell to his knees.

"Mitchell!" He shouted full-force, and in his language summoned his hunting party to emerge. Totaling fourteen in number, all males, the Balingiga escorted us the remaining one hour trek to their village. It was as though I'd emerged from a time machine. The stone altar – still there. The eternal flame, tribal god statue (with eye sockets still devoid of black pearls, thank goodness), hut configuration, all was just as I remembered it, and the grand hut replacing the church hut had been constructed just as we'd planned it.

From this hut did the warrior summon Gamay, as Wilbur stood behind me near the eternal flame surrounded by our remaining escort. The warrior lit my lighter for her, closed its lid and handed it to her, but Gamay did not take it from him. Her eyes were locked onto me, her hands clasped to her cheeks, her white teeth exposed in a grin of amazement and ultimate joy. Gamay greeted me western-style – hugging my waist, her cheek pressed to my belly, and as I separated myself enough to kneel for her she embraced me and I embraced her with tears streaming from both of us. Kisses were frantically planted from her to me and from me to her onto our cheeks, noses, foreheads and lips. And then we held each other in motionless silence, her mouth in the crook of my shoulder and neck, my mouth in the crook of hers. And as we tumbled to my left and to her right, we embraced while prone on the ground, oblivious to everything but ourselves. And had I at that moment been naked like Gamay, Gamay would have worshiped me right then and there for all Balingiga eyes to see, just as she had done back when it was forbidden, for no eyes to see.

Still, she forced me onto my back and there we stayed, my arms securing her, pressing her breasts to my chest. Too bad Wilbur had to fuck it all up.

"Uh, Hank… don't we have some business to transact?"

Not hiding my disgust, I looked up at him. "Things move slowly here, Wilbur. We're not in the States, and as of right now they don't know you from shit. So I suggest you take a seat where you're standing and catch your breath. Don't make them nervous."

He must have assumed that since he was with me he'd have no need to fear the Balingiga. Not true. And with the sudden realization that his fate rested solely upon my words, Wilbur Carson kindly sat on his butt with ashen face and eyes that said, 'I'll be good... I'll be good.'

I'd told Carson as little as possible about my tribe, partially because I had no way of knowing whether or not they'd still be here, and if so whether or not they'd be the same as when I left them, but mostly because the less he knew about them the better for me. I intended to keep him on a very short leash.

By this time all Balingiga were gathered and watching what was for most of them a bizarre occurrence – a tall white-skinned man laying on the ground hugging their queen.

"Gamay," I spoke softly. "Your people... English?"

She lifted her head from my chest, shaking no.

"Tell people... Mitchell... here." Releasing her from my grasp, I coaxed Gamay to join me in standing, and then I lifted her onto the altar. She stood and summoned them as I took a seat on the ground next to Carson, his two bags and my one set to our sides.

Gamay was thirty seconds into her speech when she first said the word Mitchell and pointed to me, at which time every Balingiga turned their heads from her. Their eyes grew wide, jaws dropped, as I stood for their inspection. Continuing with her tale, Gamay commanded their attention with every word, but when I heard the word Mitchell all heads turned simultaneously as though the tribe were watching a tennis match. Each gaze upon me brought expressions of wonder, sighs and oohs and ahs that inflated my ego a bit more than I should have allowed. But just imagine how I felt when upon the mention of my name for at least the sixth time an escort of females came to me, took me by my hands and led me to the slab of stone to join Gamay. Along the way they unbuttoned and removed my shirt.

Gamay weathered the years much better than I. Her ebony skin retains an appearance of softness, her breasts full and vital, and although her face shows faint lines near her eyes and upon her forehead, they're nothing compared to mine. My skin held together fairly well, but the hairs covering my chest, head and belly all turned white about ten years ago. Leg hair, arm hair, arm pit hair, and last I looked, crotch hair is still dark brown. My gut's in good shape, just a bit rounded, my tits are the same, they don't sag, and my dick still works. What else could a fellow my age ask for? Apparently nothing, because the Balingiga females laid me on the altar and removed every article of clothing I had on me.

With the entire tribe gathered around and Carson still sitting by our bags with his jaw dropped, Gamay worshiped me with her patented ride on my baloney pony. And to further consecrate our reunion, Balingiga females took turns orally feasting upon any part of my body to which they could gain access. Welcome home, Henry Mitchell.

A Fake Queen

Eventually, Wilbur Carson was introduced to the tribe as my friend and so was led to the altar for a getting-to-know-you party. They removed his shirt, exposing his out of control beach ball belly, and then Wilbur's western morality training took over and he fought them from stripping his remaining garments. Of course, had I not intervened they would have done it regardless and molested him with glee, but I coaxed Gamay to call her women off of him – for now. Disappointed, the females followed all other Balingiga in returning to their daily activities. Children played; men organized a hunt; women foraged the forest, while Wilbur, Gamay and I settled into the grand hut. Wilbur the prude put on his shirt and gathered our bags.

The English language was dead from lack of use, or nearly so. No generations who came after Wilma Huckabee's pearl-diving child-laborers knew a single word of it. Gamay's only son knew more than most because she'd taught him the rudimentary words of yes, no, me, you, us, them, the, and, good, bad, here, there, come, stay, go, more, less and name. Although Gamay struggled to remember what she'd learned so long ago she was able to fill me in on the important events of the past sixty years.

First item: Boban's fall from tree limb to rock. No Gamay "mix" could help because it crushed his skull. Their son is the chieftain. He makes fire like Boban did. He was our greeter in the forest, which I suspected, but since I saw no resemblance to his parents I didn't try to guess. His given name? Boban-Gamay. His name now? Boban. That's how they do it – offspring use both parent names until parent of the child's gender dies, then the name is his. It is a wonder that Boban the 2ⁿᵈ didn't kill me in the forest when I, an intruder, claimed friendship with him when I meant his father.

A daughter was born before Boban-Gamay was. Gamay-Boban lives with her man Petok in his hut with their two children. In the grand hut resides Gamay, her son and chieftain Boban, his woman Nebon and their son Boban-Nebon. As for the ages of these people I have no clue and did not ask, for here it does not matter and unless they are ancient they all look youthful.

Did you get all that? I suspect you're just as irritated with me as Wilbur Carson was after listening to Gamay's stuttering through history for what seemed hours. He was fidgety, but silent, too afraid to bring up the pearl subject lest Gamay understood what he was talking about. And so he sat there impatiently with legs crossed, nibbling on one of the power bars we'd packed and sipping the beverage Gamay served us. Tricky Gamay. Little did I know that she'd spiked my drink with one of her patented, penis-enhancing love potions, while slipping Wilbur a tranquilizing zombie-state inducer. I wonder what he was thinking as Gamay and I rolled atop the matted floor, performing every contortion imaginable in a lust-crazed orgy of making up for time lost.

Exhausted, my cock limp and begging for mercy, I laid on my side with Gamay on hers facing me. My arm cradled her ribs, my hand rubbed her spine. Her breasts pressed my belly, her nose tickled itself in my chest hairs, and her hand clutched my worn out tool that would not respond.

"Mitchell strong," she says. "Like little Mitchell."

Precious woman. She loves my dick even when limp. "Gamay pretty," I say. "Like little Gamay."

"You like man?" She pointed to zombie Wilbur. "Sleep-wake?"

"Yes. You?"

"Yes."

And so, because Wilbur Carson couldn't make the effort to endear himself to my Balingiga friends, because he was too uptight to take advantage of their generous offer to praise him as they praised me, Wilbur Carson would not be included as their honored guest. Gamay would see to that and I would wash my hands of the whole affair. Whether she intended to keep him forever in his waking sleep or poison him or torture him was no longer my concern. He had his chance and he blew it, which of course removed my only remaining stress.

I actually would have let Wilbur have his damned pearls, if he could figure out a way to get them out of the cave and onto his boat, sailing away never to be seen again. But first I needed him to acclimate himself with these people, to know and admire them as I do, for only then could he understand that telling of them to the outside world would mean their end. I needed his compassion before I could let him have his treasure. My plans were to stay no matter what, but my greatest hope had been that once Wilbur got a taste for the life he could have here – a life of unbridled sex with as many partners as he chose, a life free of any of the constraints of western civilization – that he, like I, would choose to spend his remaining days here and forget about his damn pearls, forget about anything that had to do with dollar signs.

That didn't happen. Maybe he needed more time. Maybe he deserved a second chance. Maybe a little aphrodisiac was in order. Time would tell, and with Wilbur zombified we had plenty of that. Gamay and I made plans to visit our stream for a cooling off period, but upon exiting our hut with me in the lead came a high-pitched whimper from my right.

"Back inside, pal."

The man wore western clothes similar to my Carhartts. His left hand cupped the mouth and controlled the movements of a female Balingiga.

His right hand clutched a black pistol, probably a Glock, and as he forced us back inside ahead of his hostage and himself, his eyes zeroed in on Wilbur.

"Dad, I made it. Let's go." Wilbur Carson remained in his stupor, eyes forward, unresponsive. "Dad? What the hell's wrong with you?"

Doing my best to stay between the pistol and Gamay, I spoke. "He's resting. Nothing wrong with him… just not available right now."

"Ok, Henry Mitchell. That's you. Right?"

"Yes."

"My father named me Butch. What the hell did they do to him?"

"I told you he's resting. He'll be better soon."

"This is exactly why he had me come as backup. We knew you couldn't be trusted."

As I feared, Gamay felt the need to protect her female tribesman and she charged from behind me straight towards Butch Carson, who promptly whacked her on the head with the butt end of his pistol.

"Who's that? The pygmy queen?"

Said with sinister sarcasm, it was a blessing he knocked her out so that I could lie. "No. You have their queen already."

"Where are the rest of 'em?"

"They're on the hunt. I'm sure they'll be here soon."

"Fine. We won't be. Tie that one up." There was vine rope in the corner. I secured the wrists of unconscious Gamay behind her back. "Gag her while you're at it." Another rope did that trick. "Now, get my dad, and then let's move. He's going with us even if you have to carry him. Me and queenie will take the rear. Tie her up like you did the other one. Make it easy on me." The female's hands were secured behind her and her mouth gagged. "Good job. Where's your clothes?"

"Around."

"Ok, whatever, you pervert. Take me to the pearls. And then you better fix whatever's wrong with my father or I'm gonna blast holes into you and every one of your little mongoloid pals."

With Gamay bound, gagged and out, I took Wilbur's arm and exited the hut, Butch Carson behind me holding hostage a fake queen. Balingiga men were on the hunt, women foraging, children playing in the stream, which forced us to go upstream to cross out of their sight. I knew it was doubtful that any men would be encountered, but women were scattered in all directions and with any luck we might run across one or many of them. But then again, I found myself hoping none of the women would see us either. The thought of Butch Carson shooting them down like animals gave me chills.

We crossed the waist-deep stream, me wishing I'd put on some shoes. We traversed the remaining 60 yards to the cave entrance seeing no Balingiga, nor did they see us. They weren't there. Had they been hiding I would have sensed it. Seeing that the entrance to the cave was wide open puzzled and disappointed me, for the Balingiga and I'd spent many hours sealing it with rock sixty years prior. Worse yet, a partial pile of black pearls was clearly visible just inside the entrance with the remaining pile obviously hidden in darkness. I let go Wilbur Carson's arm, and as his son and his son's hostage joined Wilbur standing three side by side, I took a few steps closer to confirm vast numbers of pearls covering the cave floor.

What a fool I'd been to think that this treasure could remain a secret all this time, to think that those with such knowledge would broadcast it in newspapers or the internet for all to see. Perhaps others knew besides the Carsons. Perhaps Simon Huckabee sent out many bottles. Perhaps Wilbur Carson enlisted not only his son to trick me, but an entire expedition. Somebody knew. Somebody had found them, brought them out of the water for transfer, and that somebody would return to collect them. But who?

I'm sure that my skin at that moment turned ashen, just as Wilbur's had done when he realized his survival amongst the Balingiga depended upon me, for I was consumed with self-loathing. In my own greed for my own treasure – the treasure of forever happiness with Gamay and her people – I brought with me the very type of men I'd vowed to keep out. Men of greed, men of exploitation, men not unlike Wilma Huckabee – that's who the Carsons were to me. *I* did it. *I* led them straight to it, and come hell or high water *I* was going to stop it.

"It's no good, Carson. You'll never take them off this island." Leaping to the cave entrance, I turned towards him and spread my feet and my hands, clasping my fingers to the rock portal.

"I found them didn't I? What's to stop me? You gambled and you lost. Now, get out of my way, old man. Put on your clothes and crawl away to die somewhere else. Don't make me do what I'd prefer not to do."

"Then do it. Get it over with... 'cause I ain't moving."

"If you insist."

He wouldn't miss. Standing four feet in front of me with the female still in his left hand clutches, he raised the pistol, aimed it to the center of my forehead, and a streak of black shot between my legs. Clearing me, a simian form charged head-first into Wilbur Carson's gut, sending him flat on his back and casting both the female and Butch aside and to the ground. The form savagely attacked Wilbur Carson's chest with forward claws and teeth, shredding his shirt, opening his skin, until Butch recovered, rushed on his hands and knees towards them, put his pistol to the form's head and pulled the trigger.

Brains, blood and skull shot a mile, the carcass still atop Wilbur Carson's chest. I rushed Butch. I kicked his gut with my shin, which sent him sprawling onto his back. I stomped his face with my bare right foot. I stomped his right arm with my bare left foot. I fell on that arm, clasping his wrist with both my hands and slamming that wrist repeatedly to the ground until Carson let go. His pistol flew, and soon it was mine.

"Don't move."

"Oh, god... get that thing off him. It ripped him to shreds."

"A well-deserved shredding, Butch." Neither Wilbur nor his attacker were moving.

"God almighty, Mitchell... help him," Butch screamed. "What the hell is that thing?"

"I don't know, but it's good and dead. Looks like Wilbur's dead, too. Hope you're happy."

It is doubtful my Balingiga warriors had ever before heard gunshot, but the unknown sound and Butch's anguished pleadings surely would bring them to us. Without them I could do nothing more than hold Butch prisoner. "Balingiga," I yelled. "Come... Boban... come!"

Boban called the name Mitchell. I repeated the name Boban. Thirty seconds later he and his warriors were there. As I held Butch Carson at bay with his own weapon, Boban cautiously approached the beast atop Wilbur Carson's chest. He took its fur-covered arm, dragged it off of Carson and left it laying belly up on the ground. One side of its face was completely gone, its other eye wide open in a macabre glare, iris blue. The beast was covered in short black hair, skin beneath milky white. Its hands and feet were not curved ape-like, but slender and human-like. Same with the spine, not humped, but perfectly straight. The length of its body was about three feet, and its penis extended from the groin to its knees. A creature like no other, this thing was a bona-fide freak show, but it was a freak show that had saved me from certain death.

"Boban," I spoke with free finger pointing to Butch. "Man, bad."

The warriors whispered, murmured, and at Boban's command they pounced on Butch Carson. They stomped and kicked him just as their ancestors did to me. They tore away his clothing. They bound him with their vine-rope, his wrists secured behind his back, and then more rope around his arms and chest. Only then did I lower the pistol. Boban showed an interest in the weapon, tried to take it from me for inspection, but I jerked it away from him.

"Bad," I said while pointing at the pistol. Entering the cave, I walked into its darkness feeling my way along the wall, black pearls punishing my bare feet. I found the vertical hole which led to the pearl-enriched waters below and dropped the pistol, waiting to hear a confirming splash.

With the female summoned from her hiding place, her wrist rope and gag cut free, two warriors lifted the carcass of beast by its ankles and wrists while the remaining tribe surrounded the now-upright Carson. The parade began its return to our village. Boban led the way. I took the rear, first kneeling beside poor Wilbur. His shirt was ripped to threads, lines of red painted the length of his chest and stomach, while tooth marks of red dented the top of his nose, both cheeks and center of his forehead. Wilbur was dead. After suspecting me of being up to no good back in 1945, after having finally found out my secret, after having found me, Wilbur spent his entire life-savings to travel thousands of miles for this. His pearls would go nowhere. Wilbur would go no further. The Balingiga left him there to rot.

Joining the tail end of our entourage, I was unable to take my eyes off of that hideous creature that killed him. Was it man or beast? The same question could rightly be asked of me, for you see, there was no doubt in my mind from where that thing had come. This wretched entity was my creation – half-pygmy, half-U.S. Navy man, and whatever self-loathing I might have felt upon reaching the cave was multiplied tenfold on the march back.

Some do-gooder I was. Wilma Huckabee had nothing on me. At least she only sought to destroy their culture. Me? In my careless lust for self-enjoyment I planted the seed to destroy their very being. "Mitchell strong. Like little Mitchell," Gamay had said not more than two hours earlier, but she wasn't referring to my limp pecker. No, Gamay spoke of this powerful and hideous creature. Had that thing mated with other Balingiga females? Were there more of their ilk still unseen?

This nauseating revelation changed everything. Living out my remaining years with these people was now impossible. Being amongst such freaks of nature perpetrated by me would certainly put a damper on my ideas of eternal bliss. Best for Hank Mitchell to go home. For Wilbur's son there would be no going anywhere. In fact, the Balingiga might just kill both of us. Fine by me.

No-name

Once crossing the stream, I bolted ahead of everybody in search of Gamay. She was awake and struggling. I quickly severed first her gag and then her wrist bindings. I kissed her, held her in my arms, and I condemned myself.

"Mitchell bad, Gamay. Mitchell sorry... hurt you."

"Mitchell bad? Then Gamay hurt Mitchell... good." She grabbed hold my nuts, squeezed them in a loving way. "Gamay tie Mitchell... hurt good."

And I do believe she would have done exactly that if not for the interruption of her son Boban. He entered the grand hut to summon her. Several Balingiga men held down the naked and chest-up Butch Carson atop the altar with his bindings intact. Females poked, prodded and pinched him with their fingers; children lightly whacked him with sticks. He was taunted. It was their playtime, until Boban and Gamay decided what was to be done with him.

Ignoring him, Gamay slowly strode towards her abhorrent offspring, her people moving aside to clear her path. As Boban and I followed her steps, she knelt beside the thing's chest, but did not touch any part of it. She observed its hideous face, the half that was still there, and stood up with a command which prompted several men to take their daggers to the corpse. They were removing its skin just as I'd seen them do the night of our monkey feast. This confused me, for right or wrong, normal or abnormal, that thing was produced by humans and the elder Boban himself had told me way back when that his people never eat people.

"Gamay?" My hands cupped her shoulders and I dropped to one knee. "Ours." I pointed to me. I pointed to her. "Why?"

"Not ours." She turned her head no. "No-name."

"No name? I live... you live... Mitchell-Gamay."

She laughed at me, covered her mouth with her hand. "No Mitchell-Gamay... Boban-Wilma... Now dead. No-name."

Holy shit! I said to myself. That bizarre creature was running around here somewhere in 1945, a result of Wilma Huckabee's first breeding experiment. Or perhaps the pitiful woman was so horny, so bored with her husband that she just couldn't resist the talents of Boban. Either way, she got the desired size for diving but apparently couldn't bear to look at something so grotesque, so she never made any more of them. And who could blame her? Somebody in her family tree must have been one step removed from Neanderthal, because that dark fur, oversized schlong and vicious demeanor couldn't have come from Boban.

Now, granted, it was a relief to know that my seed had nothing to do with the creation of no-name, and I suspect that the beast attacked Wilbur Carson not to protect me but to protect its black pearls, choosing one of the clothed men as its enemy over the naked one, but the fact remained that I did risk producing a very similar abomination when I recklessly fornicated with Gamay, and so I was justified to continue my self-loathing.

The sordid history of this unfortunate soul, according to Gamay, goes as follows: Wilma Huckabee kept her freakish son hidden deep in the cave and taught it to cherish every pearl found, thus it became her best diver and continued to dive for them after we sealed the entrance. It was Gamay and Boban who took pity on the creature, re-opening the cave after I left their village so that it could forage for food and survive. It collected pearls. It collected berries and whatever else it could find. And that is the total summation of its 60-odd-year existence.

The Balingiga did not eat its skin cooked or otherwise. Human corpses are burned – skins first, everything else later, and this is how they are sent to their god. I witnessed for the first time this ceremony right there on the spot, as the Balingiga honored the offspring of their chieftain Boban and a long-ago but never forgotten white woman. Into the eternal flame went the beast. The name of Boban, their savior, the Balingiga chieftain who'd single-handedly destroyed their enemy "Doctor Wilma" with the fire from his mighty hand, was repeatedly chanted in song. Wild dances of stomping little feet accompanied the tossing of No-name's skin into the eternal flame. With the adding of his carcass, my old original Zippo was brought from the grand hut to also be honored. The weapon of Boban, a relic from the past, engraved with the name of Mitchell, was to be my savior once again. Butch Carson committed a heinous act. He came with Mitchell, but it is not Mitchell's fault. Mitchell was tricked, and Mitchell is good to Balingiga now as he was then. Zippos says it. Boban the younger says it. Gamay says it, and so Mitchell lives.

It was not known to me that Butch Carson also was injured during the melee at the cave. No-name managed to inflict with his claw a medium-depth gash to Carson's flank, the side I didn't kick, running from below his arm pit along his ribs and nearly to his hip bone. Before our ceremony for no-name could begin, Boban ordered Carson be removed from the altar for safe-keeping inside the grand hut. Like Mitchell so long ago, Butch Carson was staked out spread eagle and naked onto the floor where Gamay took charge of his care. Her pastes would stem infection, heal his wound and cause his flesh to mend with scar nearly invisible.

I thought this a very generous act and told her so. "Like Jesus," she said upon returning from his initial treatment, and I was comforted to know that Gamay only remembered the good parts of her Christian training. Of course, it required three days for his wound to grow back together, but when she was finished with him he looked good as new. Butch Carson was fed and kept healthy, a fine specimen of Caucasian male strength humanely maintained.

The burning of No-name did not end the celebration. A feast was in order, and to honor him properly the delicacy of monkey meat was required. The first hunt, interrupted, had produced a few birds but not nearly enough for all, so Boban organized his men to seek their quarry while some women prepared what forest delicacies had already been gathered and other women went back for more. As for me, I joined Gamay in the grand hut to assist her with the mending of Butch Carson.

Such stimulating memories for me seeing Butch bound and stretched out on the matted floor, his naked body exposed and vulnerable, the sense of isolation and helplessness he felt in not knowing what these strange little people had in store for him. I remember well the youthful Gamay feeding me, allowing me to pee, crawling all over me to explore the wonders of a fully grown man, her hand massaging me, her licking, kissing, sucking and fucking me. Yes, seeing Butch this way nearly made me wish to trade places with him, except that I had business to finish first.

"Looks like you got scratched pretty good there, Butch."

"Damn you, Mitchell," he scowled while straining against his bondage, chest rising, belly sinking. "Cut me loose. Just let me get back to my boat."

"Your boat... that's exactly what we need to discuss." I looked to Gamay, who sat next to the good side of his chest, his left, with several bowls of paste mixed and ready. "Burn?" I requested.

"Yes." She handed me one bowl and I took my seat across his chest from her.

"Now, Butch, tell me how many more people know about your little folly."

"Nobody. Dad told me and no one else."

With my finger I applied a small dab of paste to the open gash along his rib cage. He howled, flinched, tried to move away from me. "Oh, god, it burns. What is that?"

"Of course it burns. It stops infection." I dotted more onto him, rubbed it deep into his wound. "How many did you say know that you're here?" He cried out from the searing pain, repeating that only he and Wilbur knew. "I must be sure you tell the truth, Butch," and I dabbed paste to the area of cut below his rib cage.

"I swear to you... please... no more. We never told another soul."

The fire of healing paste was intense, to be sure, but nothing he couldn't handle. Butch Carson's body was strong and fit for a man in his mid-forties, and I'm quite certain he could take much more punishment than the minuscule discomfort I was causing him. Besides, once the paste went to work, its searing heat subsided to a comforting warmth as its germ-killing qualities softened skin in preparation for regrowth.
No, fear is what drove Butch to answer my questions – the fear of not knowing what atrocities might await him if I didn't intervene to help him. Butch needed me, and I needed him to spill his story so I could be sure neither he nor Wilbur had blabbed about their lucrative future, their coming good fortune that turned into a nightmare.

"Tell me, Butch. How did you locate Wilbur and me?"

"He... he had me in Manila before you arrived. I put a cell phone in his carry-on... in the trunk."

"When?"

"When you two were inside the car rental... finishing up your paperwork."

"So, what about the cell phone?"

"There's a GPS chip inside."

While Gamay sat smiling as though she hinged on every word, I sat dumbfounded and wondering what the hell he was talking about. "Tell me everything, Butch." I took a section of his open skin between my finger and thumb, pinching hard. "And I mean everything... the GPS, what it means, how it works... spill it."

"Ow! Ok, ok. I'll tell you... please... no more."

I let go and prepared to listen.

"GPS is a global positioning system chip... sends a signal to a satellite and can be used like a homing system. My cell and his were like walkie-talkies... communicate back and forth. I followed you to Aparri, waited about an hour after you guys set sail, and then purchased my own boat to track you to the island."

"Great. So, Butch, where are these cell phones now?"

"Mine's in my cargo shorts... they ripped 'em off me, remember? Dad's is in his jacket... wherever that is."

It was right there in the hut with us, right where Wilbur had dropped it. Rifling through his jacket I found the cell inside a lining pocket. "I assume this is still sending its signal to a satellite somewhere?"

"Yes."

"Gamay. I go to cave. You fix."

As I made my way for Butch's clothes, I wondered if Gamay might have misinterpreted my request that she fix Butch. I intended for her to fix his wound, but she could just as easily been fucking the poor man silly as I crossed the stream.

So much for my pride in being high-tech savvy. Computers were one thing, but this shit here was all new to me. I found Butch's clothes, removed his cellular phone and brought everything he owned with me. As I entered the village, so too did Boban and his hunting party – no monkey, but plenty of fowl. No-name's feast would have to wait.

I was relieved to find Gamay dutifully applying her paste to Butch's wound and not her vagina to his cock, and with her help I communicated to Boban that we needed to make a night-time journey through the forest and to the ocean. I was dead-tired, out on my feet, but with my boots and socks covering them and my other clothes covering the rest of me, I set out with Boban and three of his chosen best to retrace my steps. To the little inlet where Wilbur and I'd hidden our boat was our destination. There, too, was Butch's boat, and we didn't retrace my steps. Boban's better path had us smelling ocean water in about 36 hours I'd guess, with one-hour stops every ten for sleep. We ate as we walked from pouches filled with berries and nuts. Water from our stream was carried in my flask.

With the distant surf in our ears, Boban found the path taken by Wilbur and me until we cleared the forest with the view of late-day sun still several feet above the horizon. Here, I stripped away my clothing and helped the men uncover both boats. I tossed Butch's phone and his clothes and their contents into his boat, brought up anchor and started its motor. Boban held the tow line from shore while his three helpers and I swam to boat side, rocks in hand to smash its hull near the water line. Hard work but it had to be done. As solid white took on cracks of black, I climbed into the boat, told Boban to let go, and eased the vessel towards open ocean. Wheel was secured with line to keep her moving forward, and then I opened the throttle midway, diving into the water as she picked up speed. She'd take on water, slowly. It might take an hour or it might take two, but boat number one would go to the depths along with an electronic device whose signal indicated a location of nowhere.

For Wilbur's boat we repeated the process, and not only did it take his phone out to sea, but also my clothing and all contents. The sun waited for us. After my swim back to shore, Boban, his men and I sat on the beach watching a lonely Ocean Master shrink to the size of a speck in the middle of that golden half-sphere, and whether it disappeared because of distance or because it literally disappeared beneath the ocean surface I cannot say, but for me there was no remorse. Henry Mitchell was here to stay. I was committed to this island, to these people, and my Balingiga brothers took great pleasure in mocking me for my tender feet on our journey home.

The Glory of Man

The tribe welcomed five very tired and hungry men with tender loving care. They fed us a succulent pig taken that very day as our main course, and then our women took us to our homes so we could sleep in comforting arms. Imagine my surprise when Gamay led me not to the grand hut, but to our own hut positioned in line at the furthest point from where she'd lived for so many years. Constructed during our absence, our hut already was filled with her possessions of bowls and mixing tools, plus the woven-leaf floor covering had been securely tacked to ground so we could wallow freely.

Nebon, wife of Boban, daughter-in-law of Gamay, ordered construction of our hut. Essentially, she kicked her mother-in-law out because Gamay finally had her own man, and according to Gamay, Nebon did not want old people messing up her home with their love-making. Ain't that just the way of it? No matter what culture you come from, children put the oldsters out to pasture first chance they get, although rarely is the reason given that the oldsters fuck too much.

No matter, now Gamay and I were free to do as we pleased, and what she pleased to do that night was to ride on me despite me being asleep much of the time. My exhaustion meant nothing to her, but the remote possibility of her bearing my child meant plenty to me, and with the language barrier between us an obstacle I managed to convey my concerns to her.

"Gamay?" I interrupted as she sat atop my pole for initial contact.

"Yes, Mitchell," she responded while bouncing on me.

"You, me... make little one?"

She stopped bouncing and took me deep into her belly, giggling. "No. Forbidden."

Ah, ha! thought I. There was a phrase that hearkened back to the bad old days, and I pressed her. "Doctor Wilma?"

"No. Us."

Already I was feeling better about this. "Before... me, Gamay... first time... forbidden?"

"Yes."

"Balingiga forbidden?"

"Yes... Gamay fix... before... Gamay fix... now."

"Always?"

"Yes."

Life is good, my friends, and my life just got a whole lot better. It could be that after Wilma Huckabee's disastrous experiment she forbade mating outside the tribe, or it could be that population control had always been a part of Balingiga culture, but either way I was off the hook. My pharmaceutical wizard came through for me again, and because my past mistakes now seemed irrelevant I could discard them and love my woman with no reservations, no guilt, which is exactly what I did throughout the night.

We were left undisturbed in our new home during most of the next morning. I certainly needed recuperation time, and with the stream being near our hut the sounds of its bubbling waters induced snoozing just as rainfall makes rolling out of bed on workdays more difficult. Snuggling with Gamay helped, too, but the time did come when our growling stomachs forced us to action. As she sauntered towards the slab of stone where community berries and nuts sat prepared for the taking, I stood outside our doorway and stretched my old bones. Funny, I didn't feel my age this morning. Despite my overland trek from ocean to village to ocean again and back to village, there were no aches, no pains, no soreness, no stiffness.

In clear sight were the two trees to which Wilma Huckabee strung me up for crucifixion. Their trunks much thicker now, but distance from one another remained ideal for properly stretching a man, and although it's doubtful my stamina could tolerate the hours of torture she put me through, on this morning Hank Mitchell was rejuvenated, recharged with a newfound energy and strength. I intended to make the most of this euphoria, for despite my best efforts there still existed the very real possibility that other men like the Carsons were headed to our island even now. At the very least investigators might soon be looking into reasons for their disappearance, trying to trace their whereabouts, and so until intruders came, if they ever came, I planned to enjoy life here to its fullest.

That *is* why I came back. Right?

After our breakfast, I reminded Gamay that I was to be punished. She had promised, and so she summoned two men to help her tie me and stake me to my traditional spread eagle on my own floor. I was taken on a trip down memory lane, as Gamay remembered to make me wait, remembered to explore every inch of me despite my moans of impatience and want. In fact, our first session of female domination inside our new home lingered much longer than in the old days, its intensity building to a fever pitch until I thought my nuts would explode even though she wasn't touching them. Not yet.

We had nowhere to go, nobody else to worry about, and we took our time reliving what once was genuine bondage. Now it was for fun, and more genuine, based on trust.

She told me I was bad. I told her I was not. She told me I must be punished. I told her to torture me at will. She placed upon my testicles a burning salve to accept my challenge. I told her I would never surrender, that none of her tortures would break me. My balls were on fire, but still I defied her. For my defiance she smeared her paste onto my throbbing cock. She told me that soon I would talk. She cruelly laughed at my tortured penis, its desire to shoot causing it to incessantly bounce upon my belly. She tortured my belly, standing on it, jumping on it, smashing my hardened cock between her dirty little feet and it. Erotic heat drove me to madness. I told her no woman could break me. She hand-slapped my penis, recharging her heat. She re-layered my balls, worsening my madness. She layered my tits. I arched my back, thrust upwards my pelvis. My tortured cock and balls fucked air, for she would give me nothing else. She dangled her tits above my face, teased me, taunted me, keeping their glorious roundness and suckable beauty just beyond my salivating tongue. She was heartless, unforgiving, without soul, and she broke me. I begged for my finish. I promised to be a good man. I promised her the world. I vowed to worship her forever, to do as she told me when she told me regardless of what she told me. I was broken and she fucked me, the heat of her paste intensifying the heat of her vaginal friction. It was hot, the hottest ever. She was hot. I melted inside her. I cried out as a madman. I cried out as an animal, a lust-crazed, sex-starved beast, for my woman had broken me – this time.

I would defy her again – next time.

To cool, we sauntered to the stream for a swim. Little ones, as she called them, were frolicking nearby and with Gamay's guidance they overcame their fear of the tall, hairy, pale-skinned human. Here on this day is also when I began learning the Balingiga tongue, for I had no right to expect them to learn any more of mine. Hours passed with me sitting upon rocks of the stream's bed, Gamay sitting on my lap, and one by one she taught me her tribal answers to my English equivalents of which she knew. Pointing at objects increased my vocabulary. I listened and I learned and all of our communication became Balingiga.

She told me that the other white man was healed. He remained staked to the floor of Boban, and he was ready. I did not ask her what that meant because I did not care.

Our trek to the ocean delayed but did not cancel the planned feast for No-name. I was invited to join Boban and his men in their monkey hunt, and upon finding some tree-dwellers I was given opportunity to make the kill with my first blow dart attempt. Missed badly, but Boban quickly followed my errant shot with one that was true, puncturing our quarry's shoulder blade and injecting its bloodstream with poison. Another of its group was targeted for my second attempt. A hit! But in its little monkey hand. Boban said better had I missed. The monkey will die slowly, jumping from one tree to another to escape, not knowing it will die regardless. Much work for his men to follow and wait.

Nonetheless, we followed and we waited, my feet toughening to where I could keep up with the rest of them, as long as they didn't go full speed. My monkey died in the crook of a branch 30 feet up, and they made me go get it. I was shown how to shimmy the truck and defy gravity. Every part of my body ached, every part of my skin was scraped and Gamay was not pleased that her man was damaged, but I got my god damned monkey. And believe me, this time I was hungry enough to enjoy it.

The surprise for me came from not knowing that the evening's celebration was not only to honor No-name, but also to thank me for my good deeds on behalf of their ancestors and them. How did they thank Hank Mitchell? The strange man who'd fallen from the sky so long ago to save them from the evil white witch? By stretching me across their stone altar, that's how.

Now, I must admit that this made me a bit wary, brought back a few unpleasant memories as you can well imagine, but they quickly disappeared when all the females laid their hands upon me. With two men each securing my wrists and ankles, tugging them towards the corners of stone, my exposed body was worshiped from head to toe with hands, fingers, lips and tongues. No more did I feel my aggravating, tree-climbing scrapes and bruises. All I could feel was their love for me. My penis, instantly erect, became a battering ram, a carnival ride, with every female taking their turn to feel its entire width and length inside their pussy holes – their warm, wet and EXTREMELY TIGHT pussy holes.

Men, just imagine it – having your body stretched naked atop an altar of stone while countless females worship you not as a man but as a god. No part of me was spared. They sucked on me, licked on me, rubbed on me, and fucked me again and again and again. All I had to do was lay there and absorb it. All I had to do was keep my dick hard for them to one at a time use as their tool. And unlike my crucifixion torture when they performed a similar worship, this time I was not drugged. Oh, don't get me wrong, I was high as a kite, but all my senses were very naturally aware exactly what was happening, every surface of my skin stimulated and praised, as each female orgasmed themselves on my hard cock.

I did not get off, not until every woman was satisfied. This was done with purpose, for I wanted my heaven to never go away. More importantly, I waited for Gamay. The Balingiga saved her for last. This was done for the same purpose, because I was her man. No, I am her man and will forever be.

With their feast ended and my orgasm complete, my tribesmen released me from their grip and helped me from the altar. I approached Gamay, lifted her into my arms, and whispered to her using her language, "Home."

"No," she says. "Man, like Jesus."

Exiting Boban's hut, an escort of Balingiga men surrounded Butch Carson. A log not unlike the one used to torture me on the altar of 1945 rested upon the back of his neck, his wrists bound with vine-rope to either end, his jaw gagged with vine-rope behind his head. They led him to the tree – the tree near what was the church hut but now is Boban's hut – the tree with branch used to stretch me on the altar so long ago. Perched upon that branch, another Balingiga warrior waited with two ropes, the ends of which he dropped to waiting companions. They sat their prisoner on his butt, his back against the tree trunk. They tied the overhead ropes to each end of his log, and the warrior perched above dropped the other ends of his ropes, leaving each singularly draped across the horizontal branch. With three warriors manning each rope, the ascension of Butch Carson began. They tugged hand over hand until the rising log forced Butch to stand. His feet left the ground. The victim moaned, his body in full suspension, as the warriors raised him six more inches upwards. And then, the ropes were tied to stakes driven into the earth.

Immediately, Carson suffered. Crucified man... like Jesus. He planted the soles of his feet to the tree trunk and raised himself, but this was a temporary respite. Balingiga warriors roped his ankles from the backside of the tree, a single rope coming from each direction with no slack allowed.

I dare say that this man's crucifixion was far more painful than mine. With his ankles separated by two feet and secured to curvature of the tree, his toes dangled six inches above ground. His arms, stretched above his head, flared into a letter V, while his chest expanded and abdominal cavity sank. And to make his situation even more miserable, the section of tree trunk that made contact with his spine just happened to curve outward, which forced his chest and belly to protrude forward as though performing a standing up morning stretch.

Now, ladies, don't get the wrong idea about me, but something about the sight of this man stretched in his crucifixion pose struck me as very erotic. Was I jealous? No, I don't believe that was it. This form of crucifixion – patibulum and stipes in Roman terms, the t cross in English – displays the naked male physique in all its glory. It exposes a man for what he is – a perfectly engineered design of strength comprised of skin, hair, ligaments, joints, bone and muscle. A naked man on the cross is the ultimate representation of power and beauty, and this is why he is the subject of countless masterpieces of art from painting to sculpture. I was proud to have the fine physique of Butch Carson represent my gender upon the cross.

Fire from the distant eternal flame cast his naked body in a warm glow, his sweat-slicked skin glimmering, sparkling. His chest exploded with power, laterals flared from his rib cage drawing a beautifully symmetric V from his arm pits to his hips. His belly defined a compact wall of strength with six horizontal lines crossing one deep-ridged and vertically-centered line from the pit of his stomach to his pelvic bone, and with each exhale of his breath those lines became bolder, his belly muscles even more glorious. His navel formed a vertical oval, the normally hidden knot of skin now slightly exposed from his resistance to his stretching, and a thin line of fur extended from his belly button to his pelvic bone, where his belly hair thickened and widened towards meeting his crotch. Here, too, was his hair dark. Thick, bushy and spiraled, his pubic hair framed his healthy phallus and testicles, and just as my X crucifixion had done to me, this man's torture caused his penis to fill with blood. It protruded forward, piercing the air as though a horizontal spear, an elongated bullet caught in a freeze frame, and it occasionally bobbed upwards, triggered by involuntary clinches in the man's scrotum.

His arms, magnificently structured, were fully expanded to support his weight, curves and bulges of his biceps and triceps evenly matched. Thick, dark and matted-with-sweat bushes covered his stretched-wide-open arm pits. A thin carpet of hair painted his sternum and pectorals. His nipples, despite their stretching were relatively small with tips raised from their center surface.

He groaned from his agony, sounds which further enhanced and dramatized his glorious masculinity. His chest heaved in his struggle for oxygen. And just as I was forced to do, this man used all his strength to lift his body for seconds at a time in order to alleviate the pressure on his chest and belly, just so he could breathe. When this happened, the beauty of everything I described was magnified tenfold. He suffered, no doubt, but Butch Carson oozed manliness. He was strong enough to take it, and all of us stood in awe of his glorious physique as he did battle with his torture of crucifixion.

For nearly an hour we watched him use his muscles in defiance, listened to his manly grunts and groans, and then Boban took Nebon into their hut. Gamay and I did the same, as did all Balingiga, leaving Butch Carson all alone to agonize in solitude for the crimes he'd committed against them.

Our New Religion

I was surprised and a bit disappointed to find next morning that Butch no longer hung from that tree. Never expected him to expire so quickly. Made me change my opinion of him. He was a poor representative of the Caucasian male, but I felt it my duty to ask Boban of Butch's passing and the whereabouts of his corpse.

A greater surprise came to me when I entered the grand hut searching for Boban, for here I found Butch Carson very much alive and once again staked to the floor.

"Hanukkah," said Boban. He held up eight fingers. "Moons come." Those same eight digits were curled and extended again. "Moons go."

Nodding my head in agreement with Boban, I then pointed to Butch. "Mitchell? Talk?"

With approval, I knelt beside the bound man's chest, cut away his gag.

"Oh, god damn, Hank. Where've you been? He raised his head to glare at me while struggling against his ropes. "Get me the hell out of here."

"Just relax, shut up and listen."

He complied, collapsed his aching muscles and remained quiet.

"I can't get you out of here. You killed one of them, so now you belong to them."

"What? That animal was one of them?"

"Yes. Don't interrupt me again. If you do as I say you might survive, but it depends on how you handle it." He started to ask, but stopped himself so that I could continue. "They're going to hang you from that tree for eight nights, keep you in here and take care of you in between. That is your punishment. After that, I don't know what their procedure is, but I'll do my best to talk them out of killing you. Make no mistake, Butch, you must do exactly as they want. Do not fight them. If I feel you can be trusted when they're done punishing you, then I will do what I can for you. Agree?"

"Wha... what have I got to do for you to trust me?"

"Realize and accept that you're never leaving this island. Realize that those pearls are worthless here, that they're never leaving this island either, so you might as well forget about 'em. Realize that your life here can be pure joy and that there's nothing more you could ever need. What do you say, Butch?"

With a deep breath and a sigh, he answered. "Ok, Hank... I'll do my best, but... but please do something for me."

"What."

"Bury my father."

"I suspect he's a little ripe by now. Animals may have eaten him for all I know."

"Please, Hank. I think about him all the time... laying out there all alone. No man deserves that. Give him a proper burial. Would ya? And say a prayer for me, for him. Ok?"

"Sure, Butch." I grabbed hold his belly with my clawed fingers, felt his power. "I'll be proud to lay your old man to rest. Now, save your strength. You've got seven more nights of torture coming."

"Thanks, Hank... I know you don't owe me a damned..."

"That's right, I don't. I'm doing it for me, Butch... for my own peace of mind, so don't fuck me over again."

And with that I gagged him and left him.

Where the mix-up between Judaism and Christianity came from I couldn't guess, but I did find it comical. Like Jesus... crucified for the eight days of Hannukah... maybe the Balingiga and I could start an entirely new religion more confusing than those already in existence. Lucky for Butch they were giving him rest periods in between. No man could survive the cross for eight days straight, at least not in full suspension the way it was being done here.

What I needed to know was what the plans were for him after his eight days were up, and for this answer I turned to Gamay. She didn't know. The Balingiga had never before dealt with any humans who'd killed a member of their tribe, and so I proceeded with my belief that only Butch could save Butch, just as I'd told him.

The stench of Wilbur Carson hit me long before I saw his carcass, carcass being the only operative word, for one or more beasts dined on his corpse until the bones were nearly picked clean. There was nothing left to bury, so I compromised. Wilbur's remains were dragged into undergrowth, covered with leaves and dirt best I cared to, and then I told god to forgive Wilbur for his mistakes. I told god to guide him towards self-improvement in his next life. I told god to tell Wilbur that his son said hello. And finally I asked god to give Butch strength and wisdom to make the right moves in the days ahead. After a quick glance inside the cave to see black pearls untouched, I said amen, goodbye. And now back to my village for some Gamay meat.

Adapting to Balingiga life brought me no pain. Honestly, there wasn't much to do, which is why most men and women spent much of their time making love. My daily lessons in learning Balingiga tongue continued with Gamay in the stream; my daily hunting techniques improved in stealth and accuracy; and my arts and crafts training had me contributing to the tribe with bowls and baskets, blowguns and darts, vine-woven ropes, leaf-woven matting, daggers, ladders, pouches, and tools needed to make any or all of these.

With them I shared my Navy knowledge of tying knots, plus my father and Uncle John knowledge of constructing tree-branch-loaded slip-knot traps. Boban and his men scoffed at this until on the sixth day of my checking a fat boar dangled upside down waiting for me to cut its throat. Nobody laughed when they dined on Mitchell's succulent pig.

Thank god Nebon chose the far end of huts for the home of Mitchell and Gamay, because Butch Carson's nightly groans of crucified torture certainly would have disturbed my sleep time. He became our after-dinner entertainment. Once we'd get him strung up the ladders would come out. Our crucified hero was washed and scrubbed, and then we'd wait for a new layer of sweat to coat his skin. That's when his body was ravished with lips and tongues, hands and fingers. Gamay and I merely watched and enjoyed the sights, because we'd been there, done that from both sides of it.

The erotic worship of the crucified man was done mostly by the women, but also a few men, which was very difficult for Butch to accept. Damned fool wanted to pick and choose, relishing females while casting off males. Boban would have none of it. Anytime Butch tried to wriggle away from one of his men, Boban jabbed him with long stick into his belly or his ribs until he behaved. By the fourth night he no longer cared. Butch was trained to accept his praise from any and all, trained to forget his inhibitions and guilt. When a mouth came calling to drain him of his manly fluids, Butch gave it freely regardless of the mouth's gender, and he learned to like it.

What Butch didn't know, nor did I, was that Boban's reference to eight moons did not mean eight moons rising. No, Boban's reference to eight moons meant eight cycles – that's quarter, half, gibbous and full, eight times.

Of course, after his initial eight nights ended and they brought him out for after dinner fun on the ninth, I looked to Boban for explanation. After having received it I planned my words for explaining it to Butch, but he never looked at me. Butch acted like he didn't know he was doing overtime. Butch was turning into a well-trained slave. Knowing what to expect, his cock was fully erect before they'd even raised him up. And this made the nightly procedure much easier for Boban's men, for no more did they have to climb the tree to string rope. Butch stood with arms extended for them to secure the log to his wrists, and each night the log was left hanging at the tree in waiting for Butch's return the next.

As for me, I never had need to speak to Butch Carson again. His tribal name was now Man-Like-Jesus.

The Balingiga knew better than I what they were doing, for by the time MLJ's ordeal was ended he no longer was a man. He was a walking-dead tool devoid of spirit, devoid of will, devoid of the ability to defend himself, think for himself or even take care of himself. MLJ was no longer a threat to any of us, just a man dependent upon us with a very handsome and masculine body to be used by anyone who cared to partake. Perhaps this is what Wilma Huckabee had done to her husband Simon to make him obedient, to make him subservient, to make him a non-entity, and perhaps the legend of the white witch was passed down to be used for the first time as punishment for the murder of No-name.

With his eight cycle of moon punishment completed, MLJ's nights were spent staked spread eagle to the floor of a brand new hut built just for him. I helped them build it. Women who had no man of their own cared for him, bathed him, fed him, used his cock if they felt like it. And some days they'd bring him out to play on the altar or let the children chase him around the village clearing just to exercise him so he'd stay fit and handsome for them, but most of the time he remained out of sight inside his hut, naked, bound and stretched spread eagle, no longer causing any harm to any person.

A crucified MLJ became part of any important celebration such as anniversaries of birth or death, and always, the anniversary of Boban the elder's triumph over white witch. Physical realities of his crucifixion force MLJ to perform for us with his flexing muscles, heaving chest, contracting belly and throbbing penis. "He is fine slab of man meat," says Gamay in our Balingiga tongue, or at least that's the closest English equivalent I can come up with.

Not such a bad life, really. We come into the world as helpless drooling babies and usually go out the same way. My life with Gamay at times makes me feel helpless, but I am her fine slab of man meat, always willing and able to do what she wants. Without her I'd be an old man ready to check out. With her I'm Captain Henry Mitchell, 22-year-old U.S. Navy stud, almost like we never skipped a beat from 1945. That's what true lust does to a man. It transcends the physical. If I had a mirror I bet I could look at myself and see that same man who heroically stood up to the tortures of Wilma Huckabee, and I bet if she tried it again I'd still emerge victorious. By god, is that a dark brown hair sprouting on my chest?

I suspect that if and when somebody from that other world finds us, they'll just write me off as some crazy old white man beyond therapy. Some lunatic geezer who can't be saved. But they'll be wrong about me, even though I won't let them know it. I have been saved. Praise be to whatever the hell started all this, I have seen the light and I'm never shutting it down.

About the Author

You might know Jasper from his audio series, Uncle Jasper's Five-fingered Bedtime Stories, available as Podcasts or downloadable as audio MP3's from his nephew's web site, Jardonn's Erotic Tales.com. Jasper's tales, both audio and written are derived from the many people he has met through the years, working-class nobodies like himself who strive to get by month to month while enjoying life to its fullest.

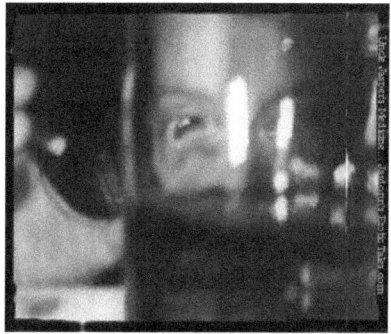

Jasper McCutcheon is also the author of:
Maggie Pie. (Nazca Plains, 2007)

Available at Goodboner.com or a local bookstore near you.